"*I'm* the one who'... "If you knew what was good for you, y... away—far away. You'd leave town just the way you came."

Devon crossed his arms over his chest. "Is that a threat?" he asked quietly.

"Yes," Todd answered, taking a few menacing steps forward. "It is."

Devon shoved him on the chest. "I've told you before, Wilkins, nobody threatens me," he said.

Todd shoved him back. "Well, there's always a first time," he retorted.

Devon pushed Todd hard, and he slammed into the table. There was a sound of shattering glass and Todd whirled around, his fists clenched. Todd gave Devon a sharp hook to the jaw, and Devon responded by punching him in the gut. Todd recoiled, wrapping his arms around his stomach. Gritting his teeth, he flew full force at Devon.

A crowd of students had gathered around to watch. "Fight! Fight! Fight!" they chanted.

Elizabeth grabbed her head with her hands, feeling as if she were caught in some horrible nightmare. "Somebody stop them!" she cried.

Visit the Official Sweet Valley Web Site on the Internet at:

http://www.sweetvalley.com

ELIZABETH IS MINE

Written by
Kate William

Created by
FRANCINE PASCAL

BANTAM BOOKS
NEW YORK · TORONTO · LONDON · SYDNEY · AUCKLAND

RL 6, age 12 and up

ELIZABETH IS MINE

A Bantam Book / April 1998

Sweet Valley High® *is a registered trademark of Francine Pascal.*
Conceived by Francine Pascal.
Produced by Daniel Weiss Associates, Inc.
33 West 17th Street
New York, NY 10011.
Cover photography by Michael Segal.

ISBN: 0-553-49229-2

Published simultaneously in the United States and Canada

Bantam Books are published by Bantam Books, a division of Bantam
Doubleday Dell Publishing Group, Inc. Its trademark, consisting of the
words "Bantam Books" and the portrayal of a rooster, is Registered in U.S.
Patent and Trademark Office and in other countries. Marca Registrada.
Bantam Books, 1540 Broadway, New York, New York 10036.

PRINTED IN THE UNITED STATES OF AMERICA

OPM   0 9 8 7 6 5 4 3 2 1

To Andrea Jean Stone

Chapter 1

Sixteen-year-old Elizabeth Wakefield's heart was pounding as she passionately kissed Devon Whitelaw. They were in a deserted field behind Sweet Valley High, but Elizabeth felt like they were in their own private paradise. The slanting rays of the afternoon sun touched her shoulders lightly, and Devon's lips were warm on hers.

Devon wrapped his arms tightly around her and lifted her in the air, kissing her all the while. Elizabeth giggled as he set her down, feeling light-headed and giddy in his intense embrace. She felt as if she had never kissed anyone before.

"My Elizabeth," Devon whispered, gently kissing her cheeks. "I've been dreaming of this moment ever since the first day I saw you."

He ran a finger through her silky blond hair and caressed her cheek lightly with the back of his

1

hand. Then he brought his lips to hers, kissing her slowly and sweetly this time.

Elizabeth's heart fluttered at his tenderness, and she closed her eyes, lost in the feeling of Devon's warm lips on hers. Kissing Devon was exciting but oddly familiar at the same time. Elizabeth had the strange sensation of being where she was meant to be. She wished she could blot out the rest of the world and stay here with him forever.

But she couldn't get rid of two nagging thoughts in the back of her mind—her twin sister, Jessica, and her longtime boyfriend, Todd Wilkins. Elizabeth had promised Jessica she would meet her by the lockers after school for a sister's night out. "It's *very* important," Jessica had said. "Don't be late." Not only was Elizabeth skipping out on their date, but she was in the arms of the guy her sister had been talking about nonstop since his arrival in Sweet Valley. And Elizabeth was cheating on Todd. He would be devastated if he could see her now.

Feeling a wave of guilt roll over her, Elizabeth pulled out of Devon's embrace. "Devon, we really shouldn't be doing this," she said. She almost didn't recognize her own voice. It was low and husky, with a breathless quality to it.

Devon gazed at her intensely, liquid fire in his slate blue eyes. "Elizabeth, you can't fight this forever," he said softly. "You know we were meant to be together."

2

Elizabeth bit her bottom lip, his words ringing in her ears. Ever since Devon had started at Sweet Valley High a week ago, Elizabeth's whole life seemed to have turned upside down. He had been assigned as Elizabeth's lab partner in AP chemistry, and he had turned out to be a total genius.

Devon had been charming her every day in class for the past week. On the first morning they met, he had mixed together a number of solutions to match her eye color, and another day he had written her a secret message in invisible ink. Last week he had even put on a fireworks display for her in the field behind school.

Not only was Devon incredible at chemistry, but he had an extremely quick mind and a wry sense of humor. Elizabeth had felt herself growing more and more attracted to him every day, and she had been desperately fighting her feelings for him. When he had asked her out last week, she had reluctantly refused. She had explained that she had a serious boyfriend whom she could never cheat on. And she had even gone so far as to send Jessica out on a date with Devon on Saturday night.

But like Devon said, there seemed to be something undeniable between them. Elizabeth felt herself thinking about him all the time. And the more she got to know him, the more she admired him. Devon was painfully handsome, but he didn't seem to be aware of it. Instead he was a bit of a loner, self-contained and self-reflective. He seemed much older than his seventeen years, Elizabeth thought. But then, he'd experienced a lot more than a normal junior in high school.

The week before, Devon had begun to open up to her. He'd been through a really hard time in the last few weeks. He had grown up in Westwood, Connecticut, but he had recently lost his parents in a car crash. After that he had moved all the way across the country to live with a woman who had been his nanny as a child. He had survived so much tragedy, yet he seemed so strong. Elizabeth sighed. There was no denying it. Devon had touched her soul.

Running an agitated hand through her hair, Elizabeth felt more confused than ever. Did this mean that everything was over with Todd? Was she ready to give him up forever?

Devon lightly cupped her chin. "A kiss for your thoughts?" he asked, a rakish grin on his face.

Elizabeth couldn't help smiling back. Devon's eyes twinkled mischievously, and tiny laugh lines appeared around the corners of his eyes.

Pushing away her troublesome doubts, Elizabeth leaned in for another kiss. For the moment she was with Devon, and nothing had ever felt so right. She'd worry about the consequences later.

"Elizabeth and Devon?" Todd exclaimed, staring at Jessica in shock. It was Monday afternoon, and he and Jessica were at Crescent Beach. She had just broken the news to him that she had caught Elizabeth in Devon's arms. As if to confirm Jessica's horrible words, the beautiful weather was beginning to turn. A few dark storm clouds had appeared on the horizon, and a light wind was picking up.

Jessica's blue-green eyes flashed angrily. "Yep, that's right. My darling, loyal twin sister is now locked in a heated embrace with Devon Whitelaw." She kicked at the ground with her foot, sending a spray of fine white sand across the beach.

"But—but that's not possible," Todd sputtered.

"Believe me, Todd, I saw them with my own eyes," Jessica said, her voice dripping with revulsion. "They were so lip locked they didn't even notice they had company."

For a moment Todd couldn't digest the information. He stared at the elaborate spread laid out on the sand, feeling a well of confusion mount in him. Todd had just spent nearly a week preparing a romantic beach picnic for Elizabeth. She was a staff writer for the *Oracle*, the school newspaper, and today was the one-year anniversary of the day her first article had been published in the paper. Todd had wanted to do something special for her, so he had put together the picnic as a surprise.

Todd had thrown himself into the preparations with all his heart and soul and had gotten all his friends involved. Enid Rollins had come over one night to give him some cooking tips, Maria Slater had made a tape of Elizabeth's favorite music, and

5

Bill Chase had helped Todd cart everything out to the beach in his surf-mobile.

Now everything was laid out perfectly on a big blanket on the sand. A beach basket was overflowing with Elizabeth's favorite foods—lobster salad, fruit cocktail, and focaccia bread. For dessert there was a homemade raspberry chocolate trifle cake and fresh strawberries. A wooden dinner tray was set up to serve as a table. A bouquet of fresh flowers in a vase stood in the middle of the tray.

Sitting on the side of the table was the final touch—Todd's gifts to Elizabeth. He had gotten a copy of Elizabeth's first article framed, and he had bought her a beautiful silver-and-diamond ring. The gifts were wrapped in elegant silver paper and topped with a matching bow.

Todd blinked. After all his efforts Elizabeth wasn't coming to his picnic? Elizabeth was with someone else? *His* Elizabeth? It just couldn't be. Todd shook his head hard. "Jess, you must finally be losing it," he asserted. "There's no way Liz would do that to me."

Jessica sank down onto her knees on the blanket, a look of sheer exasperation on her face. "Todd, why aren't you listening to me?" she asked in a frustrated voice.

A gust of wind whipped across the beach, scattering sand onto the blanket. Todd reached over and covered the picnic basket. Then he blew out the candles, sighing deeply. "I *am* listening to you,

6

but I don't think we should jump to conclusions. I'm sure this is some kind of misunderstanding." Todd squinted thoughtfully. "How do you know it was her?" he asked.

Jessica eyed him in disbelief. "Um, Todd, Elizabeth and I are twins, remember? I'd probably recognize my sister if I saw her." She stood up and held her hands in front of her, indicating an imaginary scene. "Look, I was standing in the clearing behind school, about fifteen feet away from them. They were sitting on the grass behind the softball field. Devon's hands were tangled in Elizabeth's hair, her arms were wrapped around his neck, and they didn't come up for air the whole time I was standing there."

A fierce dart of pain shot through Todd's chest at the vivid image. He felt hot tears spring to his eyes, and he quickly wiped it away in embarrassment.

Jessica shook her head. "You shouldn't waste a second crying over my two-timing twin," she declared, her voice hard. "Millions of girls would be all too happy to have a guy throw them this kind of romantic beach picnic."

Suddenly Jessica seemed to consider her own words. Her eyes softened, and she gazed into space. Then she nodded to herself slowly. "Yes, it really *is* romantic," she added. "It's a pity to let it go to waste." Jessica looked at Todd, as if seeing him for the first time. Kneeling down next to him, she reached out and put a suggestive hand on his.

Todd yanked his hand back as if he had been burned. "Jessica! Are you mental?"

Jessica shrugged. "It was just an idea."

"You're not into me, Jess," Todd said. "You're into Devon Whitelaw, Mr. I'm-too-cool. The guy you claim Elizabeth is with at the moment, remember?"

Jessica rolled her eyes. "That's my point," she scoffed. "Revenge." She stood up and paced across the sand. "If we were to start going out together, we would completely shock Liz." Jessica's eyes gleamed greedily. "She would get just what she deserves." Then she turned back to Todd, her expression softer. "Don't you want to make Elizabeth jealous?" she asked quietly, a lilting tone to her voice.

Todd was incredulous. The idea of fooling around with Jessica made his stomach turn. And playing a game wasn't going to get him anywhere. Not to mention the fact that he didn't even really believe that Elizabeth was cheating on him in the first place. There had to be some mistake.

Todd jumped up and grabbed his jacket. The only way to get to the bottom of the matter was to find out for himself. He wouldn't accept the fact that Elizabeth was with another guy until he saw it with his own eyes.

Jessica's mouth dropped open as Todd reached for his backpack and slung it over his shoulder.

8

"But what about this spread?" she asked.

Todd shook his head. "Enjoy it," he said. Then he raced off.

Jessica sat alone on the beach, shoveling lobster salad into her mouth with a serving spoon. The gourmet dish was delicious, but Jessica could barely taste it. She was so angry, she felt like she was going to burst.

The storm was really picking up now, and gusts of wind shot across the beach. Jessica stared out at the foamy green ocean, the crashing waves reflecting her tumultuous mood. She didn't know when she had been so furious. Or so frustrated. Elizabeth had double-crossed her. Devon had rejected her. And Todd was acting like a total wimp.

Jessica shoved the lobster salad away and wiped her mouth furiously with a white cloth napkin. Then she reached for a pickle and took a vicious bite out of it. The image of Devon and Elizabeth kissing in the field came back to her, causing a pain in her chest. She couldn't believe that her own sister had turned on her like this. And that Devon had chosen Elizabeth over her.

Jessica shook her head. What was going on? Devon was meant for her. She could feel it.

From the moment she had caught sight of Devon Whitelaw in the parking lot of Sweet Valley High just over a week ago, Jessica had known he was the one for her. He was strikingly good-looking and the definition of cool. Tall and lanky, Devon had longish brown hair, intense charcoal blue eyes, and full, kissable lips.

Devon was clearly Jessica's kind of guy. He was the strong, silent type, and he had a dangerous edge. He wore a brown leather bomber jacket and drove a black Harley-Davidson motorcycle. Jessica had noticed him immediately, and he had noticed her too. They had shared a moment of eye contact so intense, it had taken her breath away. Jessica was used to being looked at that way by the guys at Sweet Valley High, but she wasn't used to feeling equally captivated. In that instant she had known that this guy was the one.

Jessica had been trying to get to know him for the past week. She had deliberately "bumped" into him at school a number of times, showing up at his classes just as he was leaving them. She had invited him to the Dairi Burger for shakes one day after cheerleading practice, and she had asked him to join her at an exclusive party at Bruce Patman's on Friday night. She had even studied up on motorcycles on the Internet in order to impress him with her knowledge. But nothing had seemed to work. Devon had been cordial, but he had politely declined all her invitations. Jessica hadn't been able to understand it.

But now she did. Jessica balled her hands into tight fists, feeling the rage fire up in her again. She had asked Elizabeth to put in a good word for her in chemistry class, and Elizabeth had promised she would. But all the while her calculating twin sister had been busy seducing Devon herself.

On Saturday night everything had come to a head. Elizabeth had told Jessica that Devon would be at the Box Tree Café alone, and Jessica had gone to join him. Devon had been thrilled to see her. His eyes had lit up, and he had enfolded her in a warm hug. "I knew you would come," he had whispered in her ear.

Jessica had been thrilled too. She had been sure Devon would come around. There was no way he could resist her forever. But then she had realized that he thought she was Elizabeth—and that it was *Elizabeth* he wanted.

Not one to be made a fool of, Jessica had played along. She had been sure Devon would realize that Jessica was the one for him if he spent a little time with her. She had gone into her best Elizabeth imitation, and they had shared a passionate kiss.

That's when Devon had figured out which twin he was kissing. And he had immediately pushed her away.

"Did it ever occur to you that if you gave me a chance, you might not want to throw me away?" Jessica had persisted, using her most coquettish tone.

But Devon had just added salt to her wounds. "You're not the one I want," he had said coldly.

"You're not even my type." Jessica's cheeks burned at the memory.

Jessica raked her fingers through the sand, feeling desperate. *How could Devon prefer Elizabeth to me?* she wondered in frustration. *Doesn't he realize we're made for each other?*

Suddenly Jessica was struck with a moment of clarity. She and Devon *were* meant for each other. She was drawn to him like a fish to the ocean. And she was sure that Devon felt the same irresistible pull as she did. Jessica knew that he had experienced the electricity crackling between them in the parking lot, and she knew he had felt the searing passion in their kiss at the beach. Elizabeth was the problem. Her twin sister had confused him. She had gotten in the way and was doing everything in her power to keep Devon and Jessica apart.

Jessica stood up angrily, the depth of the deception hitting her again. Not only had Elizabeth tricked her, but she had set her up to look like an idiot. Jessica walked rapidly down the beach, staring out at the whitecapped water in wonder. She didn't know what had gotten into Elizabeth. The girl just wasn't acting like herself.

Despite their physical resemblance, from their golden blond hair to their sparkling blue-green eyes to their slim, athletic figures, the girls were completely different in character. Elizabeth was the responsible and conscientious twin, always weighing the pros and cons before making a decision. Jessica, on the other hand, tended to plunge headfirst into all her activities.

Jessica sat down at the water's edge, deep in thought. Usually Elizabeth lived according to an extremely high set of moral standards. She was a fiercely loyal friend and a highly protective sister. In fact, Jessica reflected, Elizabeth was usually *too* perfect. She was a straight-A student and actively involved in extracurricular activities. Elizabeth was always fighting for one cause or another. If she believed there was an injustice in the world, she threw herself wholeheartedly into correcting it.

Jessica, on the other hand, preferred to stir things up. If there wasn't trouble, she created it. There was nothing she liked more than getting herself into a difficult situation and then scheming her way out of it. The cocaptain of the cheerleading squad and an active member of Pi Beta Alpha, the most exclusive sorority at Sweet Valley High, Jessica led a high-profile existence at school. If there was ever a commotion, Jessica was sure to be found in the center of it.

But now the twins' roles had reversed. Elizabeth was the one throwing caution to the wind, and Jessica was the one left to pick up the pieces. Jessica sat up with a start, suddenly hit with a revelation. Elizabeth was acting like her! And Jessica didn't like it one bit.

Jessica shook her head in disgust. Elizabeth had stolen the one guy Jessica had really cared about since Christian Gorman had died in that terrible gang war. *This has gone far enough,* she thought. There was no way Elizabeth was going to outscheme her. Jessica refused to let her sister make a fool out of her. And she refused to let Devon go.

Jessica narrowed her eyes, feeling more determined than ever to correct the situation. She was going to get revenge if it was the last thing she did. The question was—how?

Jessica chewed on her lower lip, her mind clicking. The only thing to do was to fight fire with fire—and the ticket was Todd. If Todd were interested in someone else, then Elizabeth would see how it felt to be rejected. She would completely flip out and want her boyfriend back. Devon would see how fickle Elizabeth could be—that she wasn't so caring and loyal. Then he would realize that Jessica was the one who really cared about him— the one he had wanted all along.

Trailing her fingers in the cool water, Jessica closed her eyes and fantasized. She could see the situation as clear as day. *Todd falls in love with some beautiful girl. Elizabeth drops Devon and goes racing back to Todd. But it's too late. Todd is in love with someone else.*

Elizabeth is left alone. Devon is left alone. But Devon doesn't want Elizabeth anymore. Now he wants me. Sweet revenge. It could happen. Especially if Jessica helped it along.

Chapter 2

It can't be, it can't be, it can't be. Todd repeated the words to himself as he sped toward Sweet Valley High in his black BMW. A fine rain was falling, and the sleek black highway was beginning to glisten. Todd flicked on the windshield wipers, squinting through the rain to see the road in front of him.

Suddenly he caught sight of the Sweet Valley exit. He was driving way too fast. Todd flicked on his turn signal and quickly crossed the four lanes of traffic. A man in a blue Dodge slammed on his brakes and veered out of his way.

The driver blared his horn. "Hey, watch where you're going!" he yelled out the window.

Todd winced and raised an apologetic hand as he turned onto the exit ramp. Sighing, he headed onto Valley Crest Road. *That guy had every right to scream at me,* he thought ruefully. Todd was driving like a maniac. He was going to get into an accident at this rate.

Forcing himself to cut his speed, Todd started taking long, deep breaths. *Elizabeth would never do this to me,* he reassured himself. *She would never cheat on me.* Elizabeth loved him. They had been together forever, and they were going to stay together forever.

Todd reached an intersection and came to a stop. He drummed his fingers lightly on the steering wheel as he waited at the light. *There* has *to be another explanation,* Todd told himself. Maybe Jessica had made a mistake. Maybe she had misconstrued the situation. Or maybe she had lied.

Todd bit his lip. Was Jessica making all this up? It was certainly possible. Jessica was a big schemer. She had a reputation for creating outrageous situations. But what would be in it for her?

The light turned green, and Todd put his foot on the accelerator, feeling more determined than ever to get to the bottom of the situation. As he coasted down the street disjointed images of him and Elizabeth floated through his mind. He saw her cheering excitedly from the bleachers as he sank the winning basket of the championship game; he pictured them walking hand in hand across the sand at the beach, the world bathed in a silvery glow; and he saw her beautiful lips curved into a small smile as she looked deep into his eyes and told him she loved him.

16

Todd could feel his entire body heat up with anxiety. He pulled into the parking lot of Sweet Valley High and screeched to a stop. Grabbing his varsity jacket, he jumped out of the car and slammed the door. Then he took long strides across the parking lot, pulling his jacket tightly around his body.

Calm down, Todd told himself. *There's going to be a logical explanation for all of this. There* has *to be.*

His chest tight, Todd hurried down the trail leading to the softball field, heading toward the spot Jessica had described. As he reached the bottom he saw two fuzzy figures ahead, sitting on a bench. He squinted into the light rain, but he couldn't make them out. Todd felt his heart rate accelerate.

Drawing a shaky breath, Todd inched quietly through the woods. As he stepped into the clearing their profiles became visible. It was Devon and Elizabeth. And they were kissing.

Todd stumbled back a foot, feeling like he had been physically assaulted. Devon's hands rested lightly on Elizabeth's waist, and her arms were wrapped around his neck. Todd stared at them openmouthed, as if he were watching a train wreck in progress.

Todd clenched his jaw, feeling himself fill with a blind rage. He wanted to run to the field and rip that jerk's hands off his girlfriend's body. He wanted to beat him to a pulp and leave him

17

bleeding on the ground. That guy would rue the day he ever set foot in Sweet Valley.

Elizabeth giggled softly and whispered something in Devon's ear. Todd ducked back into the woods, feeling a sharp ache in his chest. It wasn't like Devon had taken Elizabeth by force. Obviously she was there on her own accord. Todd felt overcome with hurt. How could Elizabeth betray him like this? How could she throw away everything they had together?

Todd leaned against a tree trunk, taking long, deep breaths of the sweet, rainy air. Finally he felt a bit calmer. He couldn't act rashly. His pride was at stake, but so was his girlfriend. If he wanted to keep Elizabeth, he had to keep his wits about him. Devon Whitelaw looked like a forcible rival.

Todd headed back to the parking lot, one thought in his mind. *Elizabeth will be mine again,* he told himself. *I'll win her back if it's the last thing I do.*

"Um, Devon, I think we'd better go before we drown," Elizabeth said, laughing lightly.

Devon took a step back, suddenly aware of the fact that they were both wet. He had been so wrapped up in Elizabeth that he hadn't even noticed the change in weather. Now light raindrops were pattering quietly on the grass.

Devon pulled Elizabeth tightly to him. "Don't worry," he said. "I'll protect you from the elements."

Elizabeth leaned back and smiled at him. "Ah! My knight in shining armor."

A ray of sunlight peeked through the clouds, causing the grass to glitter brightly. Devon glanced at Elizabeth's smiling face, and his breath caught in his throat. She looked almost angelic. Her cheeks were flushed pink, and her bright blue-green eyes were sparkling in the rain. Tiny raindrops glistened on the ends of her eyelashes.

Devon swallowed hard, feeling his normal reserve shatter. Elizabeth Wakefield had an effect on him that no girl had ever had before.

Elizabeth cocked her head thoughtfully. "Hey, is something wrong?" she asked softly.

Devon shook his head slightly. Elizabeth was so intuitive that she sensed even the smallest changes in his mood. But he wasn't ready to share his innermost thoughts with her yet. He didn't want to overwhelm her with the intensity of his feelings. "No," Devon said finally, brushing back a strand of wet hair from Elizabeth's face. "I was just admiring you."

Elizabeth rolled her eyes, but her cheeks flushed a deep crimson. She quickly turned away from him. "C'mon, let's go," she said.

Devon took her hand, and they headed across the wet field. "Will you allow your knight to give you a ride home in his chariot?" he asked.

Elizabeth grinned. "You mean, your motorcycle?"

Devon nodded. "It's sort of a modern chariot."

Elizabeth shook her head. "Thanks, but I've got

some stuff to wrap up for the *Oracle*. I've really got to finish my Personal Profiles column before tomorrow."

Devon looked at her in admiration. The more he got to know Elizabeth, the more he found he respected her. She was smart, funny, and conscientious. Not to mention heartbreakingly beautiful. "Then I'll accompany you to the door," he said.

Suddenly Elizabeth's expression turned serious. "OK, but act normal," she cautioned him, smoothing down her hair self-consciously. "I don't want anyone to get any ideas."

Elizabeth drew a deep breath as they reached the back door of the high school. Squaring her shoulders, she marched through the door as if she were about to go into battle.

Devon grinned slightly as he followed her inside. "Do you think we're wearing signs that say Just Kissed?"

Elizabeth put her hands up to her cheeks. "Yes, I do," she said with a sigh. "I feel like I've got *guilt* written all over my face."

Devon touched her cheek lightly. "Hey, Liz, sometimes things change, you know?"

Elizabeth nodded, but her expression remained troubled.

When they reached the door of the *Oracle* office, Devon smiled at her softly. "See you tomorrow," he said. "First thing."

"See you tomorrow," Elizabeth whispered.

Devon leaned in close to kiss her good-bye, but Elizabeth backed up nervously. She looked around to make sure nobody was in the vicinity. Standing up on her toes, she kissed him quickly on the lips. "Bye," she said. Then she turned and hurried through the door.

Devon watched her disappear into the office, feeling strangely raw. As he headed down the hall he tried to make sense of his emotional state.

Devon had never felt this way about anyone before. At his old school in Connecticut he'd always had girlfriends, but none of them had ever succeeded in penetrating his heart. Devon never let anyone get close. And most of the girls he went out with ended up boring him after a few weeks. He always had the feeling they were more interested in being *seen* with him than in getting to know him. None of his relationships had lasted long.

But with Elizabeth it was different. He felt like he could trust her instinctively. He had the uncanny sense that he'd known her forever. It was like his entire trip across the country had been leading him to her.

Feeling pensive, Devon pushed open the door leading to the parking lot. He had never set much stock in fate, but he and Elizabeth felt completely right together. He had known it since he arrived in Sweet Valley and saw her for the first time. It was like two electrons that completed their atoms' outer shells and created a stable compound.

Devon walked across the wet gravel, feeling strangely elated and strangely vulnerable at the same time. As he reached his motorcycle he was struck with an awesome thought. He was in love. For the first time in his life he understood what it meant to be joined to another person. Devon slung a long leg over his motorcycle and reached for his helmet, feeling dreamy. Tomorrow seemed like a long time away.

"You. Whitelaw." Devon swung around, his wave of warm emotion stopped cold by the angry voice behind him. Todd Wilkins stood in the parking lot, his face seething with fury. His whole body was stiff and coiled, and his hands were balled into fists by his side. Devon recognized the stance immediately. It was that of an animal ready to spring.

Devon forced himself to remain calm. Elizabeth's boyfriend couldn't have possibly seen them out in the field, and there was no point in alienating him. "Can I do something for you?" he asked.

"Yes, you can," Todd spat out. "You can stay away from my girlfriend."

Devon shrugged. "That's for Elizabeth to decide," he said calmly.

Todd took a few menacing steps toward him. "I said, stay away from her." His voice was low and threatening.

Devon faced him evenly. "And if I don't?"

Todd's eyes glittered dangerously. "Then it's you

and me, Whitelaw," Todd said through clenched teeth. "And you don't know what I'm capable of when it comes to Elizabeth."

Devon's face hardened. "I don't respond well to threats," he said. Then he revved the engine and roared off, leaving Todd in the dust. *Nothing against you,* Devon thought, *but now that I've got Elizabeth, I'm not gonna let her go.*

A few hours later Elizabeth carefully pushed open the front door of the split-level Wakefield house on Calico Drive. Her lips were bruised and raw, and she could still feel Devon's passionate kisses. She had barely been able to work on her article for the *Oracle*.

When it came to her column, Elizabeth was usually a perfectionist, but today she had been too wound up to concentrate. Finally she had just printed out the piece as it was and turned it in. She had walked all the way home to calm herself, but she still felt jittery.

Elizabeth tiptoed across the foyer and headed quietly up the steps, hoping to avoid her sister. She wanted a few hours to herself—to work out her feelings and decide what to do about the situation with Devon and Todd. But as she made her way around the corner at the top of the steps, she collided right into Jessica.

"Well, look who's here," Jessica remarked sarcastically.

"Uh, hi, Jess," Elizabeth said. She continued down the hall to her room.

But Jessica waltzed in the door behind her. "You were supposed to meet me by the lockers, remember?" she asked. She was standing in the doorway, her hands on her hips.

Elizabeth's face reddened. "Jessica, I'm sorry. I forgot all about it." Elizabeth was a bad liar, and her voice wavered slightly as she spoke. "I, uh, I had to finish my article for tomorrow."

Jessica plopped down on the bed, her palms flat on the quilt by her sides. "Oh, so you were at the *Oracle* office all this time?" she asked. She crossed her legs and looked at her sister expectantly.

Elizabeth dropped her backpack on the floor. She knelt down on the rug and began pulling out her books, not meeting Jessica's eyes. "Uh-huh," she responded.

"That's funny," Jessica remarked lightly, "because I came to look for you there and I didn't see you."

"Oh, really?" Elizabeth asked. She searched desperately for an excuse, but nothing came to mind. "That *is* funny," she said finally, wanting to kick herself for being so lame. She picked up her books and carried them to her desk, steadily avoiding her sister's gaze.

"And not only that," Jessica said, her voice beginning to take on a singsong quality, "but Caroline Pearce said she'd seen you head out to the field behind school."

Elizabeth's heart began beating a drumroll in her chest. Tall, redheaded Caroline Pearce was notorious for being the class gossip. If she had seen Elizabeth and Devon together in the field, then the news would be all around school by tomorrow morning. Elizabeth forced the disturbing thought away. Caroline couldn't have possibly seen them. Elizabeth was sure she and Devon had been alone.

Elizabeth forced her voice to sound casual. "Oh, I just took a walk," she explained, waving a dismissive hand in the air. "And then I got so caught up in my article at the *Oracle* that I lost track of the time."

"Are you sure you didn't get caught up in Devon Whitelaw's arms?" Jessica asked pointedly.

Elizabeth whirled around and faced her sister. Jessica was sitting on the bed, bobbing her foot up and down in agitation. She had an accusing look on her face.

"You know," Elizabeth said softly, sinking down onto her desk chair.

"Yes, I do," Jessica responded, the anger clear in her voice. She stood up and paced across the room. "I can't believe you betrayed me like this," she said, shaking her head in bewilderment. "All this time you knew I was interested in Devon and you went after him yourself."

"Jessica, I promise, it wasn't like that," Elizabeth responded quickly. "I really didn't mean for it to happen. I tried so hard to fight my attraction for

Devon." Elizabeth gave her sister an imploring look. "You've *got* to believe me. I really tried to get the two of you together."

Jessica lifted an eyebrow. "Look, don't do me any favors, OK?" She leaned against the dresser, her arms crossed over her chest.

Elizabeth sighed and dropped her head into her hands. "What a mess," she muttered under her breath.

"So just like that it's good-bye, Todd?" Jessica asked in an aggressive tone. "Out with the reliable old four door with lots of mileage. In with the exciting new wheels?"

Elizabeth felt flustered. Was that what she wanted? Was she bored with Todd? Were her feelings for Devon real? Elizabeth shook her head, feeling totally confused. She stood up and crossed the carpet, wringing her hands. "Jessica, please, don't tell Todd," she begged her sister.

"And why shouldn't I?" Jessica asked, a challenge in her voice. "Are you intending to have them both?"

Elizabeth shook her head slowly, trying to work it out herself. No, she wasn't planning to have them both. And she wasn't planning to lie to Todd. She had to make a choice. And she had to make it quickly.

Elizabeth sat down on the edge of the bed with a sigh. She couldn't bear the thought of hurting Todd. She *did* love him. But she couldn't stand the idea of not being with Devon either. She'd tried to stay away from him, and it didn't work. "No," she said finally. "I'm not planning to go out with both of them. I just have to figure out how to tell Todd. And *what* to tell him."

"Well, it's too late for that," Jessica announced, a victorious look on her face.

Elizabeth's stomach turned. She looked at her sister in alarm. "What do you mean?"

Jessica shrugged. "Todd already knows."

Elizabeth's mouth dropped open. "You *told* him?" she gasped.

"I guess I should have been loyal to you," Jessica muttered sarcastically. She crossed the floor and sat down in the cream-colored velvet divan in the corner.

Elizabeth flinched at her sister's angry words. Jessica was right. Elizabeth couldn't expect her sister to guard her secrets when Elizabeth had stolen the guy she wanted. Elizabeth sighed deeply. "But I—I don't understand. When did you see Todd? Isn't he at basketball practice?"

"Well, for your information, lover boy Todd has spent the last week planning a picnic for you," Jessica responded evenly, flipping her hair over her shoulder.

Elizabeth's eyes widened. "Wh-What?" she stammered. "But—but why?"

"I guess you've forgotten, but it's the one-year anniversary of the first piece you had published in the *Oracle*." Jessica leaned back on her elbows. "Todd got this great idea to surprise you with a romantic picnic, and I was supposed to bring you to the beach." Jessica shrugged. "But then you didn't show up. You were busy with someone else."

A tidal wave of guilt crashed over Elizabeth. Panicked, she reached for the phone and picked up the receiver. Her heart began to pound against her rib cage as she punched in Todd's number. But when the phone started ringing, she quickly put the receiver down. She didn't really know what she was going to say. Could she actually break up with the guy she had cared about for so long? On the other hand, could she give up Devon? He had a hold on her she couldn't shake.

Elizabeth dropped her head in her hands again, tears coming to her eyes. She felt like her world was crashing down around her. "What have I gotten myself into?" she whispered to herself.

Jessica headed downstairs, shaking her head in disgust. *Elizabeth deserves to feel terrible,* she thought. After all, she betrayed Jessica, and she betrayed Todd. What did she think would happen when she played with everybody's feelings?

Jessica turned into the copper-colored kitchen to find something to eat. Her mother was standing at the stove, stirring pasta in a saucepan. Apparently she had just walked in because she was still wearing her suit from work.

Mrs. Wakefield was an interior designer, and she had been working late recently on a special project. She looked particularly professional today in a peach-colored linen suit with a cream-colored blouse. Pearl drop gold earrings and a chunky gold necklace completed the outfit.

"Hi, Mom," Jessica said, pulling open the refrigerator door. She foraged inside, looking for a snack.

"Hi, dear," Mrs. Wakefield said, placing a frying pan on the stove. "Do you want some pasta?" She poured olive oil into the pan and flicked on the burner. Picking up a cutting board, she scraped diced onions and garlic into the pan with a wooden spoon.

Jessica shook her head. "No, thanks, I already ate." Nothing looked appetizing in the fridge. She grabbed a can of soda and pushed the door shut with her foot.

Mrs. Wakefield brushed a lock of hair off her forehead, sighing deeply. "I feel terrible for abandoning you like this, but apparently my project is going to go on all week." The onions began to sizzle, and she lowered the fire. "It looks like you kids are going to have to fend for yourselves for a few days."

"Don't worry about it, Mom," Jessica reassured her. "We'll manage." She put her hands on her hips and surveyed the kitchen, looking for some junk food.

Mrs. Wakefield gave Jessica a grateful smile and ruffled her hair. "You're the best," she said. "I'll make it up to you on the weekend, OK?"

"Does that mean Chinese stir-fry?" Jessica asked. She spotted a bag of potato chips on the counter and grabbed it.

"You got it," Mrs. Wakefield said, her bright blue eyes twinkling.

Tucking the bag of chips under her arm, Jessica headed for the den. *Thought food,* she mused as she walked down the hall. Just what she needed. A brilliant idea was percolating in her head. Elizabeth was going to pay for stealing the guy Jessica had fallen head over heels in love with.

Jessica shut the door of the cozy room behind her and curled up on the sofa. The image of Devon with his arms wrapped lovingly around her sister floated into her mind the moment she leaned back into the soft cushions. Suddenly the anger flowed out of Jessica and was replaced by a nagging feeling of loss. Day and night for the past week all Jessica had been dreaming about was the moment she'd finally find herself in Devon's embrace. The moment he'd finally realize he loved her. She had to get him back. She had to find a way to make him forget about Elizabeth and realize who the real woman in the Wakefield family was.

Jessica ripped open the bag of chips and popped a few into her mouth, crunching loudly. *Don't get whiny, get even,* she told herself. Then she reached for the phone and set it down next to her. Cradling the receiver in the crook of her neck, she quickly dialed the number of her best friend, Lila Fowler.

Lila sounded out of breath as she answered the phone.

"Hey, were you in the middle of moving a mountain?" Jessica asked, reaching for her can of soda.

Lila laughed. "Something like that. My parents just bought an antique coffee table, and we were moving it into the living room."

An entire wing of the Fowler mansion had recently burned down due to an act of arson, and the Fowlers were in the process of restoring their home. The event had been particularly tragic for Lila. Her bedroom had been demolished, and she had lost all her personal possessions. Lila had gone into a deep depression at the time, but she seemed to have recovered her spirits.

"Do you want to call me back?" Jessica offered, taking a swig of soda. She set the can down on the table and grabbed a handful of chips.

"Are you kidding?" Lila responded. "This is a great excuse to get out of work. So what's up?" she asked.

"I was just wondering what Courtney Kane is up to these days," Jessica said, biting into a chip. She leaned back against the sofa and crossed her legs on the table in front of her. Courtney Kane was a friend of Lila's from the Sweet Valley

Country Club. Courtney lived in Sweet Valley, but she went to Lovett Academy, a prep school in Cedar Springs.

"Courtney Kane?" Lila said. "Why do you ask?"

"I've got my reasons," Jessica responded. She twirled the phone cord around her index finger. "Is she still moping around about her short-lived relationship with Todd?"

"Courtney's not exactly the moping type, but she's not seeing anyone right now," Lila said. "And she *is* still carrying a torch for the guy."

Jessica brightened at Lila's words. "Great," she said. "I need to talk to her."

"What's going on?" Lila asked, sounding intrigued.

"Oh, just a little matchmaking," Jessica responded vaguely. "And a little revenge. All at the same time."

"You're going to get Courtney and Todd together again?" Lila asked.

"That's the idea," Jessica affirmed, standing up with the phone held to her ear.

"What about Liz?" Lila prodded.

"My darling sister is in for a rude awakening," Jessica hissed.

"Oooh! Sounds juicy. What's going on?" Lila persisted.

"I'll fill you in on the details later," Jessica said. She walked across the shaggy carpet, dragging the phone line behind her.

Lila laughed softly. "Well, whatever it is, count me in," she said.

"You got it," Jessica responded.

Jessica hung up and sat back down on the couch, her eyes narrowed in thought. Todd and Courtney Kane—it was the perfect solution. Sometimes Jessica even surprised herself with her own brilliance.

Courtney and Todd had had a tumultuous fling some time ago. When Todd had moved back to Sweet Valley from Vermont, he had attended Lovett Academy and had dated Courtney for a while. She and Todd had lived the high life together, attending swanky parties and chichi affairs together. Courtney had been madly in love with him at the time.

But in the end Todd had gone back to Elizabeth. At a relay race between Sweet Valley High and Lovett Academy, Courtney had tampered with Elizabeth's climbing rope to make Elizabeth look bad and ensure a Lovett Academy victory. Just as Courtney had planned, Elizabeth's rope had broken and she had crashed to the ground. But what Courtney *hadn't* counted on was Todd's reaction. He had immediately run to Elizabeth's side, and he had stayed there ever since.

At the time Courtney had been steaming mad. She had been frustrated that her plan had failed, and she had been furious that Todd had chosen Elizabeth over her.

Jessica rubbed her hands together. If anyone could get Todd's attention, Courtney could. She was sophisticated and cultured, with a model-like beauty. And Jessica was sure Courtney still had a thing for Todd. The girl had been practically obsessed.

Jessica's eyes gleamed. *This just might work,* she thought.

Chapter 3

Elizabeth walked across the parking lot of Sweet Valley High on Tuesday morning, her stomach a tight bundle of nerves. She was dreading seeing Todd. Even though she had tossed and turned all night trying to work out her feelings, she had only gotten more and more confused. She still had no idea what she wanted to tell Todd.

Elizabeth heaved a sigh. She was nervous about seeing Devon as well. It would be so much easier if she could just shut off the feelings she had for him. But she couldn't stop thinking about him. Her heart pounded whenever she recalled his tender kisses from the day before.

When Elizabeth reached the door, she hesitated for a moment, wondering if she should just turn around and go back home. *Maybe I should say I'm sick and spend the day in bed,* she thought.

But then, she realized, that wouldn't solve the problem. It would only put it off until tomorrow. She couldn't hide from Todd forever. *Time to face the music,* Elizabeth thought wearily.

Elizabeth pulled open the front door and walked into the lobby. Keeping her eyes on the floor, she joined the throng of chattering students heading down the hall. If she took her lunch in the *Oracle* office, she could possibly avoid seeing Todd. The only problem was that his locker was in the same corridor as hers.

Suddenly the PA system crackled, and the principal's deep voice boomed over the loudspeakers. "Attention, everybody!" Mr. Cooper announced. "There will be a special assembly in fifteen minutes. Please head straight to the auditorium before your first-period classes."

Elizabeth breathed a sigh of relief, feeling that she had been granted a reprieve. Now she could avoid seeing Todd *and* Devon. She was sure she could hide in the crowd in the auditorium. And she wouldn't have to see Devon in first-period chemistry class either.

Swinging her backpack over her shoulder, she turned around and quickly headed in the opposite direction. When she arrived at the auditorium, she looked around nervously. The room was beginning to fill up with students, who were laughing and talking in groups. Elizabeth glanced around, searching for her friends. Then she caught sight of

Enid Rollins and Maria Slater sitting in the back row on the left side of the room.

Elizabeth waved, and Enid made a motion for her to join them. Elizabeth hurried across the room. Then she rushed up the aisle, dodging wandering students as she went.

Elizabeth arrived at the back of the auditorium, panting. "Hi, guys," she said breathlessly. Shrugging her backpack off her shoulder, she quickly took a seat next to Maria.

Maria looked funky as usual. A former child actress, Maria had a style all her own. Today she was wearing a pair of big blue overalls over a cropped white top. A wine-colored scarf was tied over her short curly hair, and silver hoop earrings complemented her lovely, mocha-colored skin. Enid looked cute as well. She had on a forest green baby doll dress that brought out the color of her eyes, and her curly reddish brown hair was pulled back in a thick green headband.

Enid gave Elizabeth an odd look. "I've never seen you so excited about an assembly before."

Elizabeth's face reddened. "Um, I'm trying to avoid Todd this morning." She shrank down in her seat, glancing around the auditorium nervously.

"Uh-oh," Maria said. "Boyfriend problems?"

Elizabeth knew that she couldn't hide anything from Maria. Maria was her oldest and most insightful friend. She had a knack for getting right to the heart of things.

Maria leaned in close. "I seem to remember you getting all excited over a certain mysterious stranger in your chemistry class who shall remain nameless. Do I see a love triangle?" she guessed.

"What?" Enid gasped.

Elizabeth hesitated. She wanted more than anything to confide in her friends. She felt completely alone in the world at the moment, and she could use some female support. Now that she had alienated Jessica, she didn't have anyone to talk to.

"Attention, everybody! Attention, everybody!" Mr. Cooper announced from the microphone in the middle of the stage. He tapped the mike a few times to make sure it was working.

"Saved by Chrome Dome," Maria whispered with a grin, employing the students' nickname for the bald principal. She waggled a finger in the air. "But don't think you're off the hook."

"Good morning, everybody," Mr. Cooper said in a loud, clear voice. "Thank you for coming. We have a big event planned for this weekend, and Mr. Russo is here to tell you about it."

Mr. Russo, the chemistry teacher, walked across the floor. A tall, older man with short graying hair, Mr. Russo had a dignified air and a welcoming smile. He was very well liked and highly respected by the students.

"Thank you," Mr. Russo said, taking the microphone from Mr. Cooper.

Mr. Russo placed the microphone in the stand.

"In light of the statewide science contest to be held in San Francisco this summer, we will be hosting a science fair on Saturday in the main field of Sweet Valley High," he announced. "All students are encouraged to participate, and science projects from all fields are welcome, including chemistry, physics, and the environmental sciences. All interested contestants should sign up in my room."

"What's the prize?" someone called out from the middle of the crowd.

Mr. Russo leaned into the mike. "The prize is an enhanced sense of self and an entry to the national competition this summer." A number of groans could be heard in the auditorium.

Mr. Russo just smiled, obviously pausing for effect. Then he cleared his throat and leaned forward again. "Which means an all-expenses-paid weekend in San Francisco, of course."

The room erupted into chatter at his words. Mr. Russo grinned as he stepped down from the mike.

"A science fair!" Enid exclaimed. "What a cool idea!" She turned to Maria, her green eyes glowing excitedly. "What do you think? Should we sign up?" Maria and Enid were science lab partners, and they'd been working on a solar energy project all year.

Maria raised her hand in the air, and the girls high-fived. "We are *so* in!"

Enid turned to Elizabeth. "What do you think, Liz? Are you and Devon going to enter?"

Elizabeth's face flushed at the mention of his name. "Uh, I don't know," she mumbled.

"Well, it looks like we've hit the jackpot!" Maria exclaimed. She turned to Elizabeth and folded her arms determinedly across her chest. "Now, *what* is going on?" she asked, a no-nonsense look on her face.

Elizabeth bit her lip and looked around nervously. "I can't talk about it now," she whispered.

"I know you have a meeting at lunch today, so tomorrow. Lunchtime. Outside. Got it?" Maria commanded.

Elizabeth nodded, smiling slightly. It felt good to know she had friends who cared. And she was thrilled to be able to get the story off her chest.

As the girls filed out of the auditorium Elizabeth couldn't help turning her mind to the science fair. There was nothing she would like better than to work on an intense project with Devon. And with Devon as her partner, she was sure they would take first place.

Elizabeth's stomach fluttered nervously as she approached the chemistry classroom. *What if everything is different with Devon now?* she worried. *What if we're uncomfortable together? What if he regrets our kisses?*

Elizabeth stood back in the doorway for a moment, taking in the room. The atmosphere was sterile and functional. Several large lab tables with steel sinks stood in the back of the class. The far wall of the room was lined with shelves containing lab supplies, and a locked door in the very back had a sign on it that read Danger: Hazardous Materials. The front half of the classroom consisted of standard wooden desks facing a large blackboard.

It was funny, Elizabeth mused, but in a short week the room had become strangely familiar. Despite the coldness of the environment, chemistry class had a homey feeling to it now. It had become her and Devon's special place. Elizabeth's stomach fluttered again at the thought of him.

Taking a deep breath, she composed herself and walked through the door. Devon was already at their lab table, mixing up some kind of potion. He gave her an intimate smile, and Elizabeth's heart skipped a beat.

"Hi," Elizabeth said softly as she slipped into her seat next to him.

Devon caught her eyes with his. "I was afraid I wouldn't get to see you today." He turned on the faucet and filled up a glass beaker with water.

"Yeah, I thought the assembly might take up the whole hour too," Elizabeth remarked. She pulled her chemistry notebook out of her backpack and set it on her desk.

"Well, it's a good thing it didn't," Devon said, "or I wouldn't have been able to finish my project." Devon turned the gas on low and set the beaker over the Bunsen burner.

"Hmmm," Elizabeth said suspiciously. "That doesn't look like our lab assignment to me." A number of beakers were lined up on the lab table in front of Devon. Each one was filled one-third of the way with a cloudy solution. A pencil with a red ribbon tied around it was laid across one of the beakers. The ribbon ran into some kind of mass in the solution.

Devon waved a hand. "No, I already finished that." He tied a paper clip around the bottom of a piece of ribbon and wound the other end around a pencil.

"So what are you doing?" Elizabeth asked, studying the mixtures with curiosity.

Devon shrugged. "Oh, just a little act of laboratory magic." Then he gave her a mischievous grin. "I wouldn't want you to lose interest."

Elizabeth smiled back, feeling the tension easing out of her body. She realized that everything was going to be OK—at least between her and Devon. He seemed to be completely at ease. Obviously nothing had changed.

Devon lifted the pencil from the beaker, as if testing the weight of it. Then he drew it out carefully. A perfect white crystal had formed at the end of the red ribbon. Holding up the ribbon in the air, he presented the sparkling rock to Elizabeth.

"But what is it?" she asked, her eyes wide.

"It's a rock candy crystal," Devon explained as she took the crystal from him. "As sweet as you are," he added with a grin.

Elizabeth laughed, enchanted with Devon's latest creation. Devon never stopped impressing her. Every day he had a magical surprise for her. When she had told him she liked the smell of roses the week before, he had concocted a special perfume that captured the scent of the flowers perfectly. The next day he had given her a bouquet of paper roses made out of rainbow-colored tissue paper. Elizabeth never knew what he would come up with next.

Elizabeth held the rock up to the light, watching it sparkle on all sides. "It's completely symmetrical," she remarked. "I guess that's the distinguishing mark of a crystal."

Devon nodded, looking impressed. "That's exactly right," he affirmed. "A crystal is just like a rock except that the molecules or atoms are arranged in an orderly array."

Elizabeth squinted thoughtfully as she studied the crystal in her hand. "So what counts is the microscopic level," she commented. She felt like she had learned more about chemistry from Devon in one week than she had learned from her textbook all year. Elizabeth lifted the rock and sniffed at it. "I can really eat this?" she inquired.

Devon shrugged. "Well, only on one condition."

Elizabeth grinned. "What's that?"

"That you agree to go to the movies with me after school," Devon said. "There's an old Hitchcock movie called *Rebecca* playing. It's one of his best."

Elizabeth hesitated. She knew she shouldn't go

out with Devon until she made a decision about Todd. It was bad enough that she had kissed Devon yesterday. It would be even worse if she started dating him while she and Todd were still officially a couple. But Elizabeth loved old movies, and there was nothing she would rather do than spend the afternoon with Devon.

"I love old movies," Devon added. He laid the pencil over one of the beakers and wound the ribbon around it until the paper clip dangled at the edge of the solution.

Elizabeth blinked, startled to hear him echoing her thoughts. She couldn't help thinking that Todd never wanted to watch the same movies as she did anymore. They used to watch old classics together all the time. But now he seemed to prefer action movies or psychological thrillers.

Elizabeth fidgeted with the ribbon in her hand. *It's just a movie,* she thought. A movie wasn't necessarily a date. After all, she went to the multiplex with her friends all the time.

"Liz?" Devon asked, touching her hand lightly.

Elizabeth bit her lip. "Well, OK," she said finally. Then she gave him a small smile. "But I have a condition too."

"Anything," Devon responded. The water was bubbling on the burner, and Devon reached forward and flicked off the gas. After setting the beaker down on a hot plate with a pair of tongs, he measured out a cup of sugar and poured it in the water. Then he picked out a long spoon from the supplies in front of him and stirred the mixture carefully.

"That you teach me how to make a rock crystal candy," Elizabeth said.

"You got it," Devon responded. He indicated the solution he was stirring. "It's really easy, actually. You start by dissolving sugar in boiling water."

Suddenly Mr. Russo approached their table and leaned in to inspect their work. Elizabeth felt her face flush. She and Devon were supposed to be working on their lab project, not flirting and making rock candy. But Mr. Russo had a warm smile on his face. "Ah, a test of crystallinity," he remarked.

Elizabeth let out her breath. Apparently neither Mr. Russo nor Devon was concerned about their lab assignment.

Mr. Russo leaned over, resting his hands over his knees. "I wanted to let you know that I signed you two up for the science fair," he told them.

"You did?" Devon asked, a perplexed look on his face.

"Well, Devon, we received your impressive records from your old school," Mr. Russo explained, his face beaming with fatherly pride. "It would be a great honor for Sweet Valley if you would participate in the fair." Mr. Russo spread out his arms. "I hope you don't mind that I took the initiative."

Elizabeth was thrilled. She looked up at Devon

with a grin. It was a great honor that Mr. Russo had thought of them.

But Devon frowned, a flicker of discomfort crossing his eyes. "Actually," he said in a soft voice, "I do mind."

Mr. Russo stood up straight, looking confused. "But Devon, it would be a terrible shame to let this opportunity pass. With your talent for the sciences, you'll be our most promising participant."

"I really appreciate the offer, Mr. Russo, but I'd prefer not to take part in the fair," Devon insisted.

Mr. Russo looked disappointed, but then he shrugged. "Well, it's your choice," he said. Then he gave them a kind smile. "But let me know if you change your mind."

After Mr. Russo walked away, Elizabeth looked at Devon questioningly. "You don't like science fairs?" she asked.

Devon shrugged, but a flicker of pain appeared in his slate blue eyes. "It's just not my kind of thing," he said.

Elizabeth was curious, but she didn't push the matter any further. Obviously Mr. Russo had hit a chord. Devon would have to open up to her in his own time.

"A science fair!" scoffed Bruce Patman at lunch. "That's the geekiest idea I have ever heard."

"This place is becoming Nerd Central," Jessica agreed.

46

Jessica was eating lunch with her friends in the cafeteria, and everybody was talking about the science fair. Winston Egbert and Maria Santelli were on the bench across from her, and Jessica's best friends, Amy Sutton and Lila, were sitting to her right. Bruce was at the head of the table, and he'd been trashing the fair for the past fifteen minutes.

For once Jessica found herself agreeing with him. Bruce was one of the richest and best-looking guys in school, and he knew it. He and Jessica usually disagreed on everything. But when it came to science, they shared the same sentiments. They both hated chemistry. They had been lab partners all year, and they both did the minimum to get by.

"I think a science fair is a great idea," Winston Egbert put in, picking up his bologna sandwich from his tray and taking a big bite out of it. Affectionately known as the class clown, knobby-kneed Winston Egbert was one of the most diligent students at Sweet Valley High.

Bruce looked at him with scorn. "I'm not surprised," he said.

"Oh, Bruce, don't be so closed minded," Maria said, coming to her boyfriend's support. Pretty, brown-haired Maria was known for taking an interest in almost everything. She was a member of the cheerleading squad, the Pi Beta Alpha sorority, and the student council as well. "Science can be fascinating. Think of Einstein. Or Marie Curie. Where would the world be without them?"

47

Bruce shrugged. "Somehow I don't think there's an Einstein at Sweet Valley High." He downed his soda and crumpled up the can.

Jessica's thoughts immediately turned to Devon. Apparently Devon was the best student ever to walk through the doors of Sweet Valley. Jessica found it hard to believe that someone with a genius IQ could still be so sexy.

She could just imagine him taking first place at the science fair, Elizabeth right at his side. The image of her true love with her own twin made her blood boil. Elizabeth and Devon would get loads of attention, and the whole school would think they were the perfect couple.

Jessica stabbed at her french fries with a fork, forcing herself to push the thought out of her mind. That would never happen, she reassured herself. Devon would never participate in a geeky science fair. He was way too cool for that.

"It's too bad they're not having a fashion fair," Lila remarked wistfully. She tucked her long brown hair behind her ear with a carefully manicured fingernail. "It would be a great excuse to go shopping." Lila sat back and crossed her legs elegantly at the knee.

"Now that's a good idea," Amy agreed. "A fashion show would be a hundred times more interesting than a bunch of dorky science experiments."

Bruce snickered. "It would be much more interesting to *look* at," he put in. He reached for his hamburger and took a big bite.

Lila rolled her eyes. "Bruce, sometimes you are *so* predictable," she said. She picked up her bottle of mineral water and took a delicate sip.

"You know, you could do something with fashion for the science fair," Winston suggested.

Lila looked down her nose at him. "Fashion is an art," she asserted. "Not a science."

Maria shook her brown curls, a thoughtful look on her face. "No, it's both. The conception is artistic, and the realization is scientific."

"Yeah, I guess that's true," Lila said, looking pensive. "Hmmm, I wonder if we could make some kind of mannequin. Or robot."

"That's it! A robot! It would be a slave to fashion!" Amy put in, her gray eyes flashing with excitement. "We could make a sort of mechanical fashion model!"

"That's the spirit," Maria encouraged them. "Winston and I are going to sign up too. We were thinking about making a solar car."

"What about a submarine?" Winston suggested.

"Or a robowaiter?" Lila put in.

Jessica looked away, tuning out the conversation. She couldn't believe how excited everybody was about this fair. Even Lila and Amy were getting into the idea. Jessica shook her head. This school was turning into a bunch of total geeks.

Elizabeth's thoughts were spinning as she headed toward the *Oracle* office at lunchtime. She didn't know what she was getting herself into. She couldn't understand why she had agreed to go to the movies with Devon, and she couldn't believe she was cheating on Todd.

Elizabeth sighed. She knew she had to talk to Todd—and break up with him. What she was doing wasn't fair to him, and it wasn't fair to Devon. But for the moment she had to get her thoughts together.

Elizabeth turned the corner and gasped out loud. Todd was standing right next to the door of the *Oracle* office, his arms folded across his chest. Elizabeth backed up a step, feeling the color drain from her face. "Todd!" she exclaimed softly.

His face was a mixture of hurt and anger. "Were you just going to avoid me and hope I'd go away?" he asked.

Elizabeth bit her lip. It was closer to the truth than she could bear to admit. She and Todd knew each other so well that he seemed to be able to read what she was thinking. A mixture of guilt and tenderness welled up in her. But she was also totally confused. Elizabeth studied Todd's face carefully. She had thought he would be furious, but he looked strangely calm.

"What's going on, Liz?" Todd asked.

Elizabeth swallowed guiltily, wondering what to say. That Devon made her see fireworks? And that Todd didn't—anymore? Elizabeth searched for a way to explain, but she found herself at a loss for words. "I—I'm—I'm sorry, Todd," she whispered finally.

"You're sorry," Todd repeated, his voice flat.

Elizabeth ran an agitated hand through her hair. "Todd—I—I didn't want to hurt you," she said in a tiny voice.

Todd's eyes softened. "Look, you have hurt me," he affirmed. "But I'm willing to call it a mistake and move on."

Elizabeth frowned. She had to tell Todd the truth, and she had to tell him now, before this situation got any more out of control. She took a deep breath and shuffled her feet nervously. "It wasn't a mistake," she whispered.

Todd winced, but then his face hardened. "Look me in the eye and say you don't love me anymore," he dared her.

Feeling challenged, Elizabeth did as he said. She stood up straight and stared directly at him. Todd looked back at her with his pained, coffee-colored eyes.

As Elizabeth gazed into Todd's familiar face a store of memories came flooding back to her. She remembered their first kiss under the big oak tree in the park; she saw them surrounded by their friends at the Dairi Burger after a basketball game; she pictured the two of them racing into the ocean at Moon Beach. She and Todd had been together for so long that he felt like a part of her now.

Elizabeth turned quickly away, feeling her

heart melt. She opened her mouth to tell him she didn't love him anymore, but she couldn't get the words out. It wasn't true. She still had strong feelings for him.

"You *do* still care about me," Todd said softly.

Elizabeth nodded and lowered her eyes. "Of course I do," she whispered, feeling more confused than ever.

Todd reached into his pocket and pulled out a midnight blue velvet box. "I bought this for you," he said.

Elizabeth's eyes widened as Todd lifted the lid, presenting her with a sparkling silver-and-diamond ring.

Elizabeth hesitated, but Todd lifted the ring out of the box and pressed it into her hand. She sucked in her breath as she admired the beautiful sterling silver band. The ring was shaped like the ends of two tiny pencils coming together. A small diamond sparkled magnificently in the center.

Elizabeth felt a fierce dart of pain hit her in the chest. Todd had picked out the perfect gift for her. The ring was exactly her taste, and it symbolized her writing. Obviously Todd had been planning to give it to her at his beach picnic. Despite herself Elizabeth slipped the band on her finger, admiring the beautiful silver ring against her creamy skin.

Then Elizabeth pulled the ring off quickly. She didn't deserve it now. She had no right to accept Todd's thoughtful gifts. She shook her head slowly. "Todd, it's beautiful, but I can't—"

"I still want you to have it—to remind you of me and how good it was," Todd interrupted softly. "And how good it could still be."

Elizabeth opened her mouth to protest, but Todd shook his head. "Just keep it," he said firmly. "I bought it for you, and I want you to have it."

Elizabeth slipped the ring into her pocket, feeling more confused than ever. What else could she do?

Chapter 4

"Lila, what do you think of this dress?" Jessica asked, pointing to a long, raw silk, gold-colored evening gown from the *Mode* catalog.

Lila leaned in to look. "Hey, that's beautiful," she said, whistling softly under her breath. She took the catalog from Jessica and studied the spread.

Jessica was hanging out with Lila and Courtney at the Sweet Valley Country Club on Tuesday after school. The girls lay stretched out on chaise lounges by the pool, catching some rays of the hot afternoon sun and ordering clothes on Courtney's cellular phone. Courtney was wearing a high-cut one-piece bathing suit that showed off her long legs. Jessica had on a new floral bikini, and Lila was wearing a simple white maillot and a wide, pale yellow beach hat.

Jessica was just waiting for a suitable break in

the shopping conversation so she could set the first phase of her plan in motion. Once she got Courtney and Todd together, she could concentrate on winning Devon for her own and making sure Elizabeth was left single.

"Court, add this to my order, OK?" Lila said. "It's called D'orée."

Courtney pushed her designer sunglasses down her nose and lifted an eyebrow. "Are you sure you don't want to just order the whole catalog?"

Lila pursed her lips. "In case you've forgotten, my entire wardrobe was recently reduced to nothing." Lila set down the catalog on a glass table by her side and reached for her suntan lotion. Squeezing a small amount onto her palm, she bent over and began spreading lotion on her leg.

Courtney raised an apologetic hand. "You're right, you're right," she conceded. She reached for the order form and scribbled down the name. Laying the form down on her stomach, she lifted her face to the sun and closed her eyes.

Lila flipped idly through a catalog called *New Age* as Jessica glanced over her shoulder, wrinkling her nose in distaste at the ultramodern fashions. Suddenly Lila stopped at a spread featuring mechanical dolls dressed in neon-colored, metallic tube dresses.

"This is great!" Lila exclaimed. "It's just the kind of thing I was thinking of for my science project." A light wind fluttered through the air, and Lila held her hat to her head.

Jessica rolled her eyes. "I can't believe that you of all people are going to be in a science fair," she stated, reaching for the glass of lemonade by her side. "Did you get hit by some nerd bug?" She leaned back and took a long sip of lemonade through the straw.

Lila laughed and shrugged. "It could be kind of fun," she maintained. "My dad said he could help me with the material for a robot. I wouldn't mind having a fashion slave at my disposal."

"What's this about a fashion slave?" murmured Courtney lazily. She was stretched out on the chaise lounge, her eyes closed and her head tilted back.

"Sweet Valley is having a science fair, and Lila and Amy are going to enter," Jessica explained quickly. She finished her drink and set it down by her side. How was she going to bring Todd into this conversation? She'd been planning on working Courtney up to it subtly, but pretty soon she was going to just blurt out her plan.

Courtney's eyes popped open. "Lila Fowler? In a science fair?" She sat up and looked at Lila in alarm. "Lila, are you OK? Do you think you've got some kind of sun poisoning?"

Lila shook her head. "Would you two stop it? You're both being extremely closed minded." Pulling off her straw hat, Lila lifted up her long light brown hair and tied it deftly in a knot on her head. Then she put the hat back on, tucking in a few errant strands of hair. "You know, Jess, you might consider joining yourself. It would be a good way to get Devon to notice you."

Jessica scowled and swung her legs over the side of the chaise lounge. "I think it's too late for that," she said.

"What do you mean?" Lila asked. She reached under her chair and felt for the bottle of suntan lotion.

"Remember that surprise picnic Todd was planning for Elizabeth?" Jessica asked. She stood up and paced along the white pavement.

Lila nodded, grabbing the bottle and sitting back in her chair.

"Well, let's just say it didn't happen," Jessica said, scuffing at the pavement with her heel. "I went to get Elizabeth to bring her to the beach and . . ." Jessica's voice trailed off as the disturbing memory returned to her.

"And?" Lila prompted. She was sitting straight up, her full attention turned to Jessica.

"And I found her making out with Devon behind the school," Jessica finished, feeling the anger rise in her again. At least she now had a conceivable reason to bring the conversation around to Todd, even though thinking about Devon was making the muscles in her shoulders knot with tension.

Lila dropped the bottle of suntan lotion with a clatter. "What! Elizabeth and Devon?"

Jessica nodded, pacing agitatedly across the ground. "Yep."

Lila sucked in her breath. "I can't believe it. Elizabeth stole Devon from you. Who would have ever thought she'd be capable of such a thing? What's gotten into her? And what about Todd?"

Jessica narrowed her eyes. *Thanks, Lila,* she thought. *A perfect intro.* "I've been wondering the same thing."

Courtney got a hopeful look on her face. "So does that mean Todd is a free man now?" she asked.

Jessica nodded in satisfaction. Courtney was reacting just as Jessica had hoped. "Yep. Todd Wilkins is as free as a jaybird."

"Hmmm," Courtney said. "That's very interesting." She reached for a tube of lip balm and applied it carefully to her lips.

Jessica crossed her arms over her chest, facing Courtney with an intent look on her face. "Courtney, are you still interested in Todd?" she prodded.

Courtney made an unconvincing attempt at looking disinterested. "I haven't really thought about him much since we broke up. Why do you ask?" She lay back in her chair and studied her nails, but Jessica could tell that inside, she was totally excited.

Jessica took a seat next to her, ready to put her plan into action. "You've never thought about going out with him?" she asked in a suggestive tone.

"Well, maybe a little . . . ," Courtney said with an excited gleam in her eyes.

Jessica rubbed her hands together. "I've got a little plan that can get us both what we want," she said.

Courtney sat up straight. "Let's hear it."

"The way I see it, this is your perfect opportunity to get Todd back," Jessica explained.

"But it sounds like he probably still wants Liz," Courtney said doubtfully.

"Haven't you ever heard of the rebound?" Jessica asked. "Todd's vulnerable. You just happen to bump into him when he most needs to see a friendly face. You look absolutely fabulous, and Todd falls head over heels in love with you." Jessica leaned in close to the girls and continued. "Elizabeth realizes what she has lost, but it's too late. This time Todd rejects Elizabeth—just like he rejected you."

Courtney's eyes lit up. "That's brilliant," she breathed.

"It's a beautiful plan," Lila chimed in, reaching for a catalog. "We need to order up something extra nice for this."

Courtney pulled her chair closer to Lila's so she could look through the catalog with her. But Jessica's work was done. She leaned back and tilted her face toward the sun. She had to make sure her tan was absolutely perfect for the next time she saw Devon. Soon Todd would have Courtney, Jessica would have her motorcycle stud, and Elizabeth would get exactly what she deserved.

Jessica licked her lips. Ah! The sweet taste of revenge.

"What a beautiful story!" Elizabeth said dreamily. She and Devon were at Casey's Ice Cream Parlor, sharing a banana split with chocolate sauce. They had just seen an afternoon matinee of *Rebecca* at the Plaza Theater in downtown Sweet Valley. The movie took place at a château on the English seaside. It was the story of a newly married couple haunted by the ghostly presence of a deceased wife.

Devon smiled. "I'm so glad you liked it," he said. "It's one of my favorite Hitchcock films."

Elizabeth dipped her spoon into the ice cream, her mind on the film. "You know, it reminds me a bit of *Wuthering Heights*."

Devon nodded thoughtfully. "Yeah, it has the same haunting, mysterious quality, doesn't it?"

Elizabeth nodded. She couldn't help noticing the glaring differences between Devon and Todd. She and Todd never really discussed movies. Todd was more interested in the entertainment value of a film than its meaning.

Elizabeth wiped her mouth on her napkin, feeling a pang of guilt for her disloyal thoughts. It was bad enough that she was having a great time with Devon—she didn't have to trash Todd in her mind as well.

Elizabeth frowned. She was being so unfair to

Todd. *What is he doing right now?* she wondered. He was probably on his way home after basketball practice, feeling completely betrayed and bewildered. Plus there was the problem of her sister. Jessica really did seem to like Devon a lot. Elizabeth cringed at the idea that she was hurting the two people who mattered most to her.

Suddenly Elizabeth felt Devon's hand on hers. She looked up to find him studying her face. "Hey, is anything wrong?" he asked softly.

Elizabeth shook her head quickly, taken aback at Devon's perceptiveness. He seemed to notice the slightest changes in her mood. "No, no, nothing's wrong," she protested. She took a bite of ice cream and forced a smile on her face.

"Hmmm," Devon said, cocking his head slightly. "I'm not so convinced about that." Then he gave her a small smile. "But I think I know how to make it better." He touched her chin lightly and leaned in to kiss her.

Elizabeth closed her eyes, and everything else went out of her mind. Devon's lips were sweet and warm, and his kiss was long and tender. He was so close that she could smell his clean, masculine scent.

Elizabeth pulled back, feeling flustered. She knew she shouldn't kiss Devon in public. She and Todd hadn't even officially broken up. It would be totally humiliating for Todd if any of their friends saw them. Elizabeth took a big gulp of ice water, wondering what had come over her. When she was with Devon, she seemed to lose all hold on her senses.

Just then the waiter appeared at their table. "Would you like anything else?" he asked, picking up their empty bowls.

Devon gave her an inquiring look.

Elizabeth shook her head. "No, thanks," she said.

"I'm definitely stuffed," Devon added.

"I know what we can have," Elizabeth said after the waiter left. She reached for her backpack and untied the string. Then she pulled out the rock crystal candy that Devon had given her that morning. "Dessert after dessert," she said, holding up the sparkling rock by its red ribbon. "It's totally decadent."

"Try it," Devon encouraged her.

Elizabeth nibbled at the edge of the rock. It was sweet and sugary. "Well, I'm very impressed," she said. "But I'm going to save the rest for later."

"Maybe I'll make you a *real* crystal tomorrow," Devon said.

Elizabeth laughed. "I'm sure you'd be capable of it, but I think candy is more my style."

As Elizabeth's thoughts turned to science class her expression became more somber. She was sure that Mr. Russo had touched on something serious this morning, and she wondered what it was. She looked at Devon inquisitively. "So, why exactly don't you want to be in the science fair?" she asked.

Devon glanced down for a minute. He seemed to be weighing something in his mind. Then he looked at her and began to talk. "Well, actually I got a lot of unwanted attention at my old school because of my, um, ability in math and science," he explained softly.

Elizabeth gazed at him thoughtfully. "What do you mean, unwanted?"

Devon shrugged. "I'm a behind-the-scenes kind of guy. I do my thing because it interests me, not to impress other people, you know?"

Elizabeth nodded. She knew exactly what he meant. She felt the same way about writing and journalism. Elizabeth threw herself completely into her work, but she liked to keep a low profile. She enjoyed reporting on news, not making it. Elizabeth bit her lip. She and Devon had so much in common, it was beginning to scare her.

"And all the attention didn't do a thing for me," Devon continued. "The teachers were just interested in their own glory, and the students were all jealous." He shrugged. "It was like I was some kind of trophy for the school, but all the kids hated me."

Elizabeth wrinkled her nose in distaste. "I wouldn't like that kind of attention either."

Devon picked up his water glass and downed the contents. "I was hoping to be able to make a new start here," he explained as he set the glass down on the table. "I didn't want to be the star again."

Elizabeth put her hand on his. "I don't blame you," she said softly. Elizabeth was disappointed that they wouldn't be in the fair together, but she completely understood Devon's decision. And she felt closer to him than ever.

"Courtney, stand still!" Lila commanded as she carefully twisted a French braid into Courtney's long chestnut-colored hair.

"I *am* standing still," Courtney whined.

She shifted uncomfortably while Lila poked and prodded her with bobby pins and brushes. The girls were in Lila's bedroom, preparing Courtney for her first encounter with Todd. Lila and Jessica had spent the past half hour dressing her. Courtney never braided her hair, but Lila had insisted that Todd liked the innocent look. Courtney sighed impatiently. She was beginning to feel like a Barbie doll.

"Ow!" Courtney exclaimed as Lila stabbed her with another bobby pin. "Watch those things! They're like instruments of torture."

"Beauty has its sacrifices," Lila said dryly. "Hey, Jess, can you hand me that barrette?"

"Gotcha, chief," Jessica said, reaching for a gold clip on Lila's dresser.

Courtney sighed.

Lila twisted the braid up onto Courtney's head

and fastened it with the barrette. Then she stood back to examine her work. "There! Perfect!"

"Finally!" Courtney exclaimed, stretching out her neck and rubbing her shoulders.

"Now take a look," Jessica said, leading Courtney to the antique full-length standing mirror in the corner.

Courtney sucked in her breath. Jessica and Lila had completely transformed her. She was wearing a long, wraparound black skirt of Lila's with a scoop neck, ivory-colored Lycra T-shirt. Her hair was swept up elegantly on her head, a few loose curls framing her face. It was a tasteful outfit that still managed to show off her figure.

Courtney looked at her image in satisfaction. The girls had done a great job dressing her up. She was sure their plan would work now.

Ever since Jessica had brought up Courtney's short-lived relationship with Todd, the whole affair had come flooding back to her. She could feel the hurt and the humiliation as if it had happened yesterday.

Courtney had been madly in love with Todd, and she had thought they were the perfect couple. But it turned out that Todd had been playing with her the whole time. Courtney's father was a vice president at Varitronics, Todd's father's computer chip company. Apparently Mr. Wilkins had thought it would look good if Todd dated the daughter of one of the VIPs of his company. And Todd had just

66

been trying to make Elizabeth jealous. As soon as Elizabeth came back into the picture he had dropped Courtney like a hot potato.

But somehow the embarrassment hadn't changed the strength of her feelings for Todd. She still wanted him as much as ever, and Jessica was right. This was the perfect time to swoop in for the kill.

Courtney smiled wickedly into the mirror. There was no way Todd could resist her now.

Chapter 5

Todd trudged across the field after basketball practice on Tuesday afternoon, feeling despondent. Elizabeth's painful words had been echoing in his head all day, and they came back to him now, tormenting him. "It wasn't a mistake," he heard her say in a whisper. "It wasn't a mistake." Todd squeezed his eyes tight, feeling as if a razor sharp dagger had pierced his heart.

He shifted his gym bag on his shoulder, trying to digest the reality of the situation. Elizabeth was in love with somebody else. She didn't care about him anymore. Todd sighed deeply. Was it possible? Could their entire relationship be erased in a second? In a kiss?

Todd walked around the side of the building and stopped short, feeling his heart begin to sound a drumroll in his chest. Elizabeth was heading across the parking lot toward him. *She must be looking for me,* he thought. She must want to apologize, to tell him that *he* was the one she really loved after all.

Then he blinked as he realized his mistake. It wasn't Elizabeth. It was Jessica, and she was with Lila. Todd kicked himself for being so stupid. Jessica was the last person on earth he felt like talking to. He was in no mood to hear about her revenge fantasies. That wouldn't serve any purpose at all. All that mattered was that he had lost Elizabeth. And that he had to find a way to get her back.

Todd had turned to head in the other direction when he noticed a third girl with Jessica and Lila. His mouth dropped open as he recognized her. It was Courtney Kane, and she looked more beautiful than ever. She had changed since he saw her last. She seemed softer somehow and more refined. Her hair was pulled back, with a few soft tendrils around her face, and her elegant skirt rustled lightly around her legs. She was holding her head high, floating across the parking lot like a queen.

Todd stood rooted to the spot, his mouth hanging open. He hadn't seen Courtney since their fling, and he had thought he would never see her again.

Courtney waved and gave him a small, warm smile. "Hey, Todd, how are you?" she called.

Just as he was about to respond she said, "See

you." Then she turned and continued across the lot. He could hear the girls laughing together as they headed toward the twins' Jeep.

Todd stared after her in surprise. He thought Courtney hated him. After their disastrous breakup she had told him she never wanted to speak to him again.

Before the girls got into the car, Jessica looked back at him and mouthed a word. "Revenge," she said.

Todd cocked his head, considering her advice. Revenge wasn't the answer, but maybe Jessica was on the right track. Maybe it was time to move on after all.

"Jessica, *please* don't be angry with me and Devon," Elizabeth begged on Tuesday evening. She spread her hands wide. "When I'm with him, it feels as if it's just meant to be."

Jessica tried to squelch the flare of anger she felt and gave her twin a forced smile. "I'm not angry," she said. *I'm too busy getting even*, she added silently.

The girls were alone in the kitchen, cleaning up from dinner. Since Mrs. Wakefield was working late this week, Elizabeth had baked vegetable lasagna for the whole family. Mrs. Wakefield had been thrilled to find supper prepared. She offered to do the dishes, but Elizabeth had shooed her parents away. "We'll take care of it," she offered.

71

Mrs. Wakefield had smiled appreciatively. "You're an angel."

Jessica rolled her eyes as she cleared off the table. If only her mother knew what an "angel" Elizabeth really was. She wondered what her mother would think if she was aware of the fact that Elizabeth had betrayed her sister, cheated on her boyfriend, and lied to everybody about it.

Elizabeth picked up a stack of plates from the counter and began loading them into the dishwasher. She glanced at Jessica worriedly. "Are you *sure* you're not mad?" she asked.

Jessica shrugged. "It's no big deal," she said casually. *Yeah, right,* she thought. *So you grabbed the love of my life right out from under me. Why would I be mad?* She picked up a sponge and began scrubbing the table viciously.

Elizabeth breathed a sigh of relief. "Oh, I'm so glad you understand," she gushed. "I was worried that you would hate me forever."

Elizabeth shut the door of the dishwasher and turned the dial. It roared to life, filling the room with a soft hum.

"Of course I understand," Jessica said, trying to keep the edge out of her voice. "Obviously you and Devon were meant for each other." *Like peanut butter and caviar,* she added to herself. She crossed the Spanish-tiled floor and squeezed out the sponge into the sink.

Elizabeth filled up a teakettle with water and

put it on the stove to boil. She bit her lip thoughtfully. "It's insane," she said. "But I really *do* feel like we're meant for each other." She opened the cupboard and reached for a pair of teacups. Then she added two mint tea bags to the saucers. "We have everything in common. He's an incredible person—intelligent, funny, and really deep as well. It's like I've been waiting for him all my life. . . ." Elizabeth's words trailed off. She leaned against the counter, a dreamy look in her eyes.

Jessica gritted her teeth. This was getting to be too much. It was one thing for Elizabeth to ask for her forgiveness, but it was another for her to get all starry-eyed in front of her. Elizabeth didn't have to add salt to the wound.

"So, what do you think of this whole science fair thing?" Jessica asked, hoping against hope that she was right about Devon and he hadn't agreed to participate with her queen of the nerds sister.

Elizabeth's brow furrowed. "I'm not entering," she said. "Devon wasn't interested."

Yes! Jessica thought. Elizabeth and Devon working together on a project would have undoubtedly thrown them together even more than they already were. At least Devon wouldn't be seeing Elizabeth 24/7.

"Why didn't Devon want to do it?" Jessica asked, knowing that he was just way too cool for it.

Elizabeth looked pensive. "Well, he told me,

Jess, but it's kind of personal. I don't think he'd want me to tell *everyone*."

The kettle began to whistle, and Elizabeth jumped with a start. Shutting off the burner, she carried the teakettle to the table and set it down on a hot plate.

Jessica sat down, determined to contain her anger. She couldn't believe how insensitive Elizabeth was being, acting as if she and Devon were a private, tight couple. She had to bite her tongue to keep from lashing out. But if she wanted her plan to succeed, she would have to be patient.

She was also beginning to come up with an idea of how *she* could get to spend some extra time with Devon and convince him that she was just his type. But first she wanted to twist the knife into Elizabeth a bit.

Jessica dipped her tea bag into her cup and looked up at her twin. "Too bad for Todd, huh?" she said, weighing her words carefully. "He looks like he's just lost his best friend." Jessica lifted her teacup to her lips. "And I guess he has," she added.

Elizabeth winced at her sister's words. "I know," she said. "I feel terrible about it." She shook her head, her blue-green eyes clouded with worry. "I never would have thought he'd take it like this. I thought he would be furious with me. But instead he's being completely understanding. He wants to just call it a mistake and forget about it." Elizabeth picked up her cup and took a sip.

"I guess you should respect him for that, huh?" Jessica asked, blowing on her tea to cool it down. "He's willing to rise above his feelings."

Elizabeth nodded sadly. Then she set down her cup and leaned in closer to Jessica. "He gave me a ring today," she confessed.

"Oh, really?" Jessica asked, as if she hadn't helped Todd pick out the ring. "What kind of ring?"

"It's a silver band shaped like two pencils coming together." Elizabeth sighed deeply. "It's such a personal gift. Todd really knows me."

Jessica cocked her head, a sudden idea popping into her head. "Where is it now?" she asked. She sat back and crossed her legs, bringing her cup to her mouth.

"It's sitting in my jewelry box," Elizabeth admitted, a guilty expression on her face. "I know I should give it back," she said. "But I'm afraid to hurt him even more." Elizabeth reached for a cookie and bit into it dejectedly.

Jessica affected concern. "Poor Lizzie, you do still care about him," she said.

"Of course I do," Elizabeth answered quietly.

"It's hard for you to think of him all alone," Jessica went on.

Elizabeth nodded sadly.

Well, he won't be for long, Jessica thought.

Todd tossed off his covers and flipped onto his back, unable to find a comfortable position. He had been trying to sleep for the past hour, but all he could think about was Elizabeth.

She was so present in his thoughts that he felt as if she were there with him. He could feel the softness of her skin under his palm and the silkiness of her golden hair as he ran his fingers through it. He smelled her familiar scent, a mixture of roses and wildflowers. And he saw her smiling at him, her lips curved into a small half smile.

Todd groaned and flipped onto his side. *Elizabeth, where are you now?* He imagined her with Devon, taking a midnight walk on the beach. He saw her kissing him in the moonlight, locked in a passionate embrace. Todd punched the blankets, feeling a surge of violence well up inside him. What did this guy have that he didn't have? Why had Elizabeth chosen Devon over him?

Elizabeth, you're making a mistake. Todd spoke to her in his mind. *We're meant to be together—you and me. We always were. And we always will be.*

Todd rolled over onto his back and stared at the ceiling. He knew with certainty that he and Elizabeth were destined for each other. She was just swaying for a moment, he reassured himself. That could happen with couples who had been going out for a long time. But he was going to get her back. If it was the last thing he did.

Todd closed his eyes, dreaming about how it would be when they were together again. He imagined her enfolded in his arms, whispering her regrets.

Todd, I'm so sorry. I don't know what came over me. I know now that you're the one for me.

Shhh, Todd would reassure her. *It's OK. It's all in the past now.* And then he would kiss her. They would kiss long and tenderly, like they had so many times before.

Suddenly Todd sat bolt upright, blinking in surprise. The face in his daydream had shifted. For a moment he hadn't been kissing Elizabeth but Courtney Kane. It was Courtney's face he had seen, and it was Courtney's lips he had felt on his.

Todd sat back against the wall, frowning. Was he interested in Courtney? Did he want to go out with her again? Or did he just want to get back at Elizabeth?

Todd narrowed his eyes, carrying the fantasy through. What would happen if he dated Courtney again? Would Elizabeth get jealous like she had the last time? Would she realize her mistake and want him back?

But then he shook the image out of his head. No, that was Jessica's style, playing those kinds of games. Elizabeth was no game player—not when it came to things that were important and deep. Todd sighed. He was just going to have to hope that Elizabeth would remember why they were so special together. He was going to have to have faith that she'd come around on her own.

❖   ❖   ❖

"So how did your date go?" Nan Johnstone asked Devon after dinner. Nan placed a large glass bowl of fruit cocktail in the middle of the round kitchen table and set a jug of hot apple cider next to it.

Devon smiled. "It was great," he said enthusiastically, digging into the dessert. "Nan, the more I get to know Elizabeth, the more I'm convinced that she's the one for me."

In a few short weeks Nan had become Devon's closest friend. A middle-aged woman with thick gray hair and bright blue eyes, Nan ran a preschool in Sweet Valley. She was a warm, understanding woman with a big heart. Nan had been Devon's nanny when he was growing up in Connecticut, and his happiest childhood memories were linked to her.

"That's great," Nan responded. "What did you do?"

"We went to see an old Hitchcock movie," Devon said. *"Rebecca."* He poured out two mugs of cider and passed one over to Nan.

Nan got a wistful look on her face. *"Rebecca,"* she said softly. "That's one of my favorite films. I remember seeing it as a child." Nan cocked her head. "And did Elizabeth make a decision about her boyfriend?"

"That's the problem," Devon said, sighing. "She's having trouble letting go."

Nan looked at Devon carefully, a serious expression in her penetrating blue eyes. "I guess you can understand that," she remarked.

Devon nodded slowly. He knew Nan was referring to his trouble getting over his own difficult past. His parents' death had left him with a lot of anger and a lot of resentment. Nan never made judgments, but she had a way of making insightful remarks that often led Devon to work out his own problems.

Devon took a sip of cider and stared into space thoughtfully. Devon's parents had been absent during most of his childhood. His father had been an international financier and his mother had been a professional socialite. They had spent most of their time visiting clients and attending high-society affairs. Nan was the one who had taken care of him while his parents were flying around the country on business or social calls.

But one day Nan abruptly decided to leave. Devon had been devastated. "It's better this way," she said simply. She promised to keep in touch. But she never wrote at all. In the beginning Devon had written her weekly letters, but eventually he stopped trying to reach her. Her departure had left a gaping hole in his life. Devon's teen years were spent mostly alone.

When Devon's parents were killed in a car accident in Geneva, he barely noticed their absence. In fact, he was glad to be on his own at last. But his father's will stipulated that Devon had to find a suitable guardian in order to collect his inheritance, so he had traveled across the country looking for a guardian. His first stop had been the home of his young cousins in Ohio. He had thought the Wilsons were the perfect normal family, but it turned out they were only interested in his money. His next stop had been his uncle Pete's place in Las Vegas. Uncle Pete hadn't had any interest in Devon's inheritance, but he had set him up to fence stolen goods.

Just when he felt he had hit rock bottom, Devon received an unexpected letter from Nan. At first he had been wary of her intentions. After all, she had ignored him for all those years. But Devon was out of options, so he had gotten back on his bike and headed for Sweet Valley. When he had arrived at Nan's, she had greeted him with open arms and tears in her eyes. It turned out that she *had* written him over the years, but his parents had returned all her letters.

Devon rested his chin on the back of his hand, contemplating all he'd been through. He was furious that his parents had kept Nan's letters from him. They had caused him years of unnecessary pain. And now that they were gone, he could never get an explanation or an apology.

Devon caught Nan's eyes. She was sitting patiently, letting him think things through. "It's hard to let go of anger," Devon said quietly. "I don't know how to get over the fact that my parents kept your letters from me."

Nan looked at him sympathetically. "I don't

blame you for resenting that. But don't you think there was a reason for their actions?"

Devon shrugged. "I guess they were jealous of our relationship."

"And what does that tell you?" Nan asked.

"That they did love me, in their own way," Devon answered with a frown.

"That's right," Nan said softly. "They were scared I would replace them." Nan stood up, picked up their plates, and carried them to the sink. "Devon, try to understand," she said, turning on the water. "Your parents were very important people with very busy lives. But they *did* care about you, and they tried to be the best parents they could be."

Devon nodded thoughtfully. What Nan was saying made sense. His parents had tried to give him a proper childhood, but they were egotistical people with their own problems and their own concerns. Devon had to learn to accept them for their strengths and their weaknesses. And he had to forgive them for the mistakes they had made.

Nan leaned over and kissed him on the cheek. "Don't be too hard on yourself," she said softly. "It will take a while." Then she walked to the kitchen door and said good night.

Devon sat quietly after Nan had left the room, deep in thought. It would be a long time before he was able to completely let go of the past, but he felt that he had made a lot of progress. He was more peaceful than he had been in years. For the first time in his life, he felt like he had a home. It was as if Sweet Valley and Elizabeth Wakefield had been waiting for him all along.

Devon cupped his mug of cider in his hands. He thought of Elizabeth's golden smile and her beautiful ocean blue eyes. All he wanted to do was make her happy.

Suddenly Devon smiled to himself. He had an idea how he could do that.

Chapter 6

Devon arrived at school early on Wednesday morning. He wanted to get to chemistry before the class started to work on their lab assignment from the day before. When he got to the door of the classroom, he was surprised to find Elizabeth already there. She was alone in the room, and she was intent on some project of her own.

Devon paused in the doorway, watching her work. Her hands covered by a pair of thermal gloves, Elizabeth was opening a bottle of acid under a fume hood. She looked lovely as usual. She was wearing a pair of faded blue jeans and a pale yellow cotton sweater. She usually wore her hair back in a loose ponytail, but today it fell in soft waves around her shoulders.

Elizabeth was clearly hard at work. Her body was tensed, and her face was scrunched up in concentration. Biting her lip, she carefully poured the smoky liquid into a beaker. Her silky golden blond hair fell in a curtain over her face, and Elizabeth flipped it back impatiently.

Curious to know what she was up to, Devon crossed the room to their lab table. Now Elizabeth was lowering some kind of spongelike metal into the beaker with a pair of tongs. She was so wrapped up in her work that she didn't notice his presence. Reaching for a bottle of potassium chloride, she added a spoonful of powder to the mixture. A cloudy vapor rose from the beaker with a hiss, and Elizabeth backed up quickly, waving the smoke away. Suddenly Devon realized what she was making. She was forming an organometallic complex out of platinum.

Elizabeth consulted her chemistry book. "Crystals of potassium hexachloroplatinate are formed by dissolving a platinum sponge in a mixture of sulfuric acid and hydrochloric acid," she muttered under her breath.

"And adding a spoonful of potassium chloride," Devon finished for her.

Elizabeth looked up, startled. "Devon!" she exclaimed.

"Guilty as charged," Devon responded, taking a seat next to her.

Elizabeth quickly covered the beaker. "I wanted to surprise you," she complained, looking disappointed. "Now, don't watch."

Devon held both hands up in a gesture of sur-render. "OK, OK," he agreed, turning his face away. He pulled his chemistry book out of his leather satchel and opened it to the lesson from the day before. It covered electromagnetic waves and infrared light and their effect on chemical compounds. Pulling out his lab report, Devon began writing up the hypothesis for their lab as-signment.

Fifteen minutes later Devon had finished the assignment. He shut the chemistry book and capped his pen, setting it on the report. Drumming his fingers on the table, he began whistling softly. Out of the corner of his eye he could see Elizabeth working diligently. She was adding drops of base to the mixture to neutralize the acid.

"Devon!" Elizabeth scolded him, waggling her index finger. "You're cheating!"

Devon grinned. "Who? Me?"

Elizabeth shook her head in mock disapproval. Using a dropper bottle, she squirted a few drops of the solution onto a piece of litmus paper. The lit-mus paper turned from red to light blue, indicating that the acid had been neutralized.

Looking satisfied, Elizabeth set the beaker aside. Then she reached for another beaker sitting on the corner of the table. Lifting off the alu-minum foil covering, she peeked inside to examine her results. "It worked!" she exclaimed.

Elizabeth set the glass container on the table between them. "Look," she said proudly. "I mixed this up about an hour ago."

Devon leaned in close to see. A diamond-shaped crystal had formed at the bottom of the dish. It was amber colored and smooth on all sides. Devon whistled softly under his breath. "Hey! That's great," he exclaimed, impressed. "You've made a perfect crystal compound."

Elizabeth smiled. "Well," she said modestly, "I *do* have the world's best teacher."

Elizabeth reached forward and turned on the water in the steel sink in front of them. With a pair of tongs she drew the stone out of the dish and held it under the stream. Then she shut off the faucet and shook off the excess water.

Elizabeth dried off the stone and held it palm up. The amber crystal sparkled brilliantly in the fluorescent yellow classroom lights. She rubbed it with a dust cloth and handed it to Devon. "Here," she said. "This is for you." Her cheeks flushed a light pink, and she looked away quickly.

Devon held the golden diamond drop up to the light, feeling touched. Nobody had ever made a gesture like this before. His parents had always given him store-bought gifts, and his previous girl-friends had usually expected him to do the gift giving.

Devon touched Elizabeth's hand. "Hey, thanks," he said softly. He rubbed one of the smooth sides of the stone with his thumb. "This will be my good luck charm."

Elizabeth smiled, the dimple in her left cheek deepening. "That's what I was thinking."

Suddenly the bell rang, signaling the start of class, and students began filing into the classroom. Mr. Russo came in a few minutes later and took his seat at the lab table in the front of the classroom.

"OK, everybody, settle down," Mr. Russo said, holding up a hand. When all the students had taken their seats, Mr. Russo continued. "Today we're starting a new lesson: thermodynamic processes and thermochemistry."

A few groans could be heard from the back row, and Mr. Russo smiled. "Don't worry. You've still got time to finish up your lab reports on electromagnetic waves." He squinted as he consulted a schedule in front of him. "How about half an hour? Does that sound fair?"

A number of students in the front row nodded.

"OK, good," Mr. Russo said, clapping once. "Let me know if you've got any questions." He scraped back his stool and stood up.

Soon a low din filled the room as the students began working together in pairs. Mr. Russo walked down the first row, pointing out problems and answering questions.

"I'm glad we finished the assignment," Elizabeth said. "It'll give me some time to clean this up." She gestured at the mess her experiment had made.

Devon helped her put everything away and then pulled his stool up to the table. "I've got a surprise for you too," he said.

"Devon, you must have run out of surprises by now," Elizabeth protested. She ticked off the items on her fingers as she spoke. "Let's see, so far you've duplicated my eye color, made a bouquet of flowers, put on a fireworks display—"

Embarrassed, Devon cut her off. "No, no, it's nothing like that," he said quickly. "It's just . . ." Devon hesitated for a moment. "I thought maybe we *should* enter the science fair after all."

Elizabeth blinked in surprise. "Really?" she asked.

Devon nodded. "We can tell Mr. Russo today that we changed our minds. I'm sure he'll be psyched."

But then Elizabeth frowned. She narrowed her eyes and looked at him carefully. "Devon, are you *sure* you want to do this?" she asked softly.

Devon grinned. "Sure, I'm sure," he said. "After all, you're the one creating metallic crystal complexes. If we win, I'll just blame it on you."

Elizabeth's eyes lit up. "Oh, Devon, that's great," she exclaimed. "This is going to be really exciting." She reached for her chemistry book and opened it to the table of contents. Then she ran her index finger down the list, a thoughtful look on her face. "So what do you think we should do?" she asked.

Devon leaned in close and rubbed his hands together. "Well, I happen to have a little idea. . . ."

Jessica took one last look in the mirror of the girls' bathroom and smiled at her reflection. Her hair was brushed back conservatively, and she was wearing a lot less makeup than usual—just some lipstick, blush, and mascara. She was wearing a plaid miniskirt with a white top, low-heeled sandals, and a pair of diamond stud earrings. The effect was lovely. She was still Jessica, but less outrageous. Exactly what she was going for. It was time to put Operation Win Devon Back into effect.

The bell rang, and Jessica jumped. She reached into her bag, pulled out her chemistry book, and opened it in front of her. Then she walked out into the hall, trying to appear as if she were studying the text while discretely keeping an eye out for Devon. She knew he'd be coming out of Mr. Collins's classroom any second.

In an instant he was there. Jessica's breath caught in her throat. He was so gorgeous. His long brown bangs flopped over his forehead, and his gray T-shirt hugged his muscular chest. Jessica froze for a moment, almost forgetting her plan. Then someone bumped into her side, and she was shaken out of her thoughts.

"Wake up, Wakefield. You've got work to do," she muttered. Ducking her head and staring at her book, she walked straight for Devon like a heat-seeking missile until she slammed right into him.

"Hey! Watch it!" he exclaimed. Then he seemed to notice it was Jessica who had collided with him, and his eyes softened slightly.

"Devon! I'm so sorry," Jessica said, feeling a genuine blush rise to her cheeks. He had such a deep effect on her. "I was just studying, and I didn't see you."

Devon leaned against the wall and crossed one ankle over the other. It was unbelievable to Jessica that he could make every simple movement sexy.

"What're you studying?" Devon asked.

Jessica smirked. She could've written the script for this. "Chemistry," she answered, holding up the book. "It's not my strong point, and I have a huge exam coming up."

"Really?" Devon asked. "Have you asked Liz to help you? She's incredible at it." His slate blue eyes sparkled when he mentioned her sister. Jessica had *not* wanted Elizabeth to be part of this conversation.

"Uh, well, Liz is kind of busy, you know, with the *Oracle* and everything," Jessica improvised. "I wouldn't want to bug her. But this test is going to be a killer. I don't know what I'm going to do."

Devon shifted slightly and seemed to consider her words. *Come on,* Jessica urged. *Be a gentleman, already.*

"I could help you if you want," he said finally.

"You'd do that?" Jessica asked, flooding her voice with disbelief and gratitude. She looked up at him through her thick lashes and smiled.

"Yeah, I mean, I could tutor you or whatever," Devon said, stuffing a hand into his pocket.

"That would be great," Jessica said. "How about today after school?"

"Um . . . OK. Do you want to meet me at the school library? Say around three o'clock?" Devon asked, pushing himself away from the wall and smiling down at her.

Jessica's heart flopped as she stared at his beautiful grin. "I'll be there," she said breathlessly.

"OK. I'll see you then," Devon said, lifting a hand in a slight wave as he walked away.

Jessica watched his retreating back and grinned in triumph. Once Devon saw how studious and intelligent she was, he would realize that she had everything to offer and Elizabeth was just a boring old stick-in-the-mud. Sure, she might have to spend the rest of the afternoon talking about chemistry, but she was certain she'd be able to turn the conversation to more interesting topics every now and again.

Topics like me and Devon and our beautiful future, Jessica thought. She turned on her heel and walked excitedly back to her locker.

"OK, girl, give," Maria demanded on Wednesday at noon.

"We want the whole scoop," Enid chimed in.

Elizabeth was having lunch with Maria and Enid in the outdoor eating area. It was a perfect southern California day. The sky was a clear robin's egg blue, and the air was warm and balmy. The girls were sitting in a secluded spot of the lawn under a white oak tree.

Elizabeth looked around to make sure that nobody was in the vicinity. The picnic tables were full of chattering students, and a few kids were stretched out on the grass, enjoying the sun. Bruce Patman was sitting with some members of the tennis team across the lawn, but they were too far away to be able to hear the girls' conversation.

Convinced that nobody was within earshot, Elizabeth turned back to her friends. "You guys promise to keep this top secret?" she asked anxiously.

Enid rolled her eyes. "As if you have to ask." She pulled the lid off a container of raspberry yogurt and licked it.

Elizabeth nodded. "You're right." She leaned in close to the girls. "Well, I think I might be falling in love with Devon Whitelaw."

Maria lifted an eyebrow. "Uh-oh, I see trouble." She reached for her lunch bag and pulled out a falafel sandwich with pita bread and a bag of potato chips. Cupping the sandwich in both hands, she lifted it up to her mouth and took a big bite.

"Isn't Jessica after him?" Enid asked, dipping a spoon into her yogurt.

Elizabeth raked a finger through her hair. "Yeah, it's a big mess." Sighing, she picked up her salad and put it on her lap.

Maria wiped off her mouth with a paper napkin, squinting thoughtfully. "Does Devon know how you feel?" she asked.

Elizabeth blushed. "I think so. I think our kiss on Monday afternoon gave it away."

"What?" Enid exclaimed.

"Oh, boy," Maria muttered.

"What about Todd?" Enid asked.

"Well, apparently he saw us kissing," Elizabeth said with another sigh. She leaned back against the tree trunk, set her salad on the ground, and drew her knees up to her chest. "I told him I wanted to be with Devon, so I guess we've broken up, but it's not really official yet." She lifted a forkful of salad to her mouth, forcing herself to chew and swallow.

"Poor Todd," Enid put in, tucking a loose curl into her headband. "He went to all that work for your beach picnic." She rubbed a green apple against her shirt.

Elizabeth shot Enid a look. "Enid, I'm already being crushed by guilt. Do you have to rub it in?"

Enid raised an apologetic hand. "Sorry, sorry," she said quickly.

"Speak of the devil," Maria said suddenly, looking across the lawn.

Elizabeth turned her head quickly, following the direction of Maria's gaze. Todd was crossing the lawn alone, his gym bag slung over his shoulder.

Todd caught her eyes with his, causing a strange current to travel through Elizabeth's body. Then she watched his gaze go down to her hand. Obviously he was looking for the ring he had given her. Elizabeth suddenly felt terribly bare. Biting her lip, she looked away quickly and buried her hand deep in her lap.

Just at that moment she noticed Devon coming across the lawn toward them from the other direction. Elizabeth inhaled sharply, feeling overwhelmed.

"When it rains, it pours," Enid muttered under her breath.

Elizabeth glanced nervously back in Todd's direction. He had stopped and was glaring at Devon. Elizabeth glanced over at Devon again, who seemed to have changed his course slightly so that he would have to pass right in front of Todd.

The hair on the back of Elizabeth's neck stood on end. What was he doing? Was he trying to rub Todd's nose in the fact that he was coming over to sit with her? As Devon passed Todd, Elizabeth saw their eyes lock. The fierce anger on both their faces made her stomach turn. Todd's whole body became rigid, and for a moment Elizabeth was afraid the two boys might attack each other.

No, she told herself, shaking her head slightly. *They would never do anything like that.*

A moment later Todd turned and walked stiffly

away. She sighed in relief. But then a black cloud of guilt descended on her. *If only Todd had someone else too,* she thought sadly.

"Hi," Devon said softly, crouching down in front of them. He had a slice of pepperoni pizza in one hand and a can of soda in the other. Elizabeth glanced back at him nervously, forcing a smile.

"I'm Devon," he said, introducing himself to Enid and Maria.

"Hi, I'm Enid," Enid responded. "This is Maria."

Maria stuffed her lunch bag into her canvas book bag and scrambled up. "And we were just leaving," she said. She nudged Enid with the side of her foot.

"Huh?" Enid asked. "Oh, right!" she said. Jumping up, she grabbed her lunch bag and her backpack. Maria took her hand and tugged on it.

"See you guys later!" Enid called over her shoulder.

Devon knelt in front of Elizabeth, carefully studying her face. She was clearly disturbed. Her forehead was creased, and her eyes were troubled. He had seen the way she watched Todd walk off. *Why doesn't that guy just let her go?* Devon thought in frustration.

He leaned forward and kissed her lightly on the cheek. "Guess who I just bumped into—literally," he said, hoping to get her mind off her ex.

"Who?" Elizabeth asked weakly.

"Your lovely twin," Devon said, crossing his legs Indian style. "She's been having some trouble in chemistry, so I offered to help her after school."

"You did?" Elizabeth looked incredulous. "I mean, I didn't know she was having that much trouble. Why didn't she come to me?"

"She said you'd been busy and she didn't want to bother you," Devon answered. "I figured if I tutored her a few times, it would be one less thing you had to deal with."

"That's thoughtful of you, Devon." Elizabeth looked as if she were choosing her words carefully. "But do you think it's a good idea to spend time alone with her when she has a crush on you?"

Devon's eyebrows shot up. "Liz! Are you jealous?" he asked playfully.

"No!" she answered a little too quickly. "I just don't want you to lead her on. She's been hurt enough already."

Devon took a bite out of his pizza. "I think I can send the right signals so she knows it's not a date," he said.

"You don't know my sister," Elizabeth mumbled, hanging her head slightly.

Devon swallowed and looked at her warily. She really looked upset. "Enough about Jess. How are you doing?" he asked.

"I'm good," Elizabeth responded. She smiled, but Devon could see the sadness in her eyes.

With a slight sigh Elizabeth picked up her half-eaten salad and placed it on her tray. She reached for her sandwich, but then she set it back down again.

Devon lifted her chin and looked her in the eyes. "You know, sometimes people have to move on," he said.

Elizabeth nodded. "I know," she said. She plucked a piece of grass listlessly. "It's just . . . it's just . . ." She spread her hands in a wide gesture. "I feel so awful about Todd."

"I don't blame you," Devon said sympathetically. "It's tough to break up with someone. Especially when you've been together for a long time."

Elizabeth glanced at him quickly, a guilty expression on her face. Then she bit her lip and looked down. Wrapping her arms around her knees, she rocked slowly back and forth.

Devon set down his slice, feeling suddenly insecure. "You *did* break up with him, right?" he questioned.

"Yes, I did," Elizabeth responded. "At least I *think* I did."

Devon frowned, his chest tightening with anxiety. Maybe Elizabeth wasn't sure she wanted to go out with him now. She said she had feelings for him, but perhaps that wasn't enough. Maybe she was still in love with her old boyfriend. "You think you did?" he prodded.

"Todd knows about us," Elizabeth explained. Her words were so quiet that they were barely audible, and Devon leaned in closer to hear. "I told him that it wasn't a mistake." Elizabeth clenched at the grass with her fingers, giving Devon an intense look. "I know that you're the one for me."

"And you're the one for me," Devon responded softly. He shifted over and took a seat next to her. He hated to see her in so much pain. "Elizabeth, if you need some more time . . . you know, to sort stuff out, I'll understand."

Elizabeth looked up at him, a grateful, loving look in her shimmering eyes. For a minute Devon almost wished he could take back his words. He didn't know what he'd do if Elizabeth told him she didn't want to see him.

"That's so sweet, Devon," she said, reaching out to touch his cheek. "But it's the last thing I want. I've decided to be with you, and that's what I'm going to do."

Devon grasped her hand and kissed it lightly. She smiled, then turned back to her lunch.

Leaning back against the tree, Devon breathed a sigh of relief. It was great to know that Elizabeth had chosen him. But he still knew that until Todd was off the radar screen, Elizabeth wouldn't truly be his.

Chapter 7

Jessica tapped her foot on the thickly carpeted floor of the library while she waited for Devon to arrive. If he didn't get here soon, she wouldn't have much time to work her charms on him before she had to get outside and execute the next phase of her Todd and Courtney plot. Jessica cast a glance at the clock and sighed. All of this scheming was exciting, but it was beginning to get stressful.

"Hey, Jess."

Jessica felt a pleasant tingle rush down her spine at the sound of Devon's voice behind her.

"How did you sneak up on me?" she asked in a low tone. Her eyes had been trained on the door for the last five minutes at least.

"I got here a while ago, but I was checking out some books in the science section," he said as he slid into the chair next to hers. "Sorry I'm late."

"That's OK," Jessica said with a smile. Inside she was puzzled. Devon was flipping through boring science texts when he could've been here with her? He must *really* be into this whole chemistry thing.

"So let's get to work," Devon said, pulling his chemistry book from his leather saddlebag. Jessica almost shivered with delight. He was so cool, he didn't even carry a backpack. "What chapter are you on?" Devon asked.

Jessica froze. Chapter? She had no idea what chapter her class had been studying. Her mind whirled back to her chem period earlier that day. "We're, uh, working on heat energy releases," she improvised, hoping she'd strung the words together correctly.

"OK," Devon said, running his finger along the table of contents. "That's chapter eight." He started to flip the pages.

"Right. Chapter eight," Jessica said, nodding enthusiastically. He was all business, wasn't he? Well, they'd just see about that. "Devon," Jessica began in a whisper. "Thank you so much for helping me with this." She leaned over and touched his forearm flirtatiously.

Devon stared at her hand for a moment, then moved his arm away. "It's no problem, Jessica," he said. Then he chuckled. "Actually I wasn't surprised to find out that chemistry wasn't your thing."

"What do you mean?" Jessica asked, her brow knitting.

"You. I mean, you're obviously not the most . . . scientific person on the planet," Devon said offhandedly, looking at her out of the corner of his eye.

Jessica felt her blood start to boil. Was Devon insulting her intelligence—right to her face?

"Not like Elizabeth, right?" she asked, crossing her arms over her chest.

"Right," Devon said with a nod, his eyes skimming the first page of chapter eight. Jessica noticed he was studying a colorful picture of an erupting volcano. It completely reflected her own emotions.

"Devon Whitelaw, you are so clueless!" she shouted, standing up and grabbing her bag.

"Shhh!" the librarian cautioned from the other side of the room.

"Jess. I didn't mean—" Devon's eyes were wide with shock.

"Save it. I know exactly what you meant," Jessica fumed, ignoring the harsh looks of the library staff. "For your information, your precious Elizabeth isn't as perfect as you think she is. You think you're so smart, but let me give you a piece of advice." She slung her bag over her shoulder and looked down at Devon defiantly. "Don't turn your back on her for a second, or she'll be twisting the knife in you before you can say 'traitor.'"

With that, Jessica squared her shoulders and

marched out of the library, leaving Devon and his totally baffled expression behind.

Todd dribbled down the basketball court at full speed on Wednesday after school. He was alone in the newly renovated gymnasium, trying to work off some of his hurt and anger. He had been on the court for over an hour, and he was putting himself through a merciless workout. Even though he was just wearing a pair of light cotton shorts and a T-shirt, his whole body was drenched in sweat.

When he reached the backboard, he jumped high in the air and sank the ball smoothly in the hoop. Grabbing the ball, he dribbled back in the other direction and dunked it again. Then he ran around the twenty-foot range and performed a series of fancy jump shots. The ball swished through the hoop each time.

Elizabeth would be impressed if she could see me now, Todd thought. But then, she had no interest in seeing him anymore. She was with Devon Whitelaw, Mr. Motorcycle. Todd thought of how Devon had left him in the dust Monday afternoon and their encounter at lunch today and could feel his face flush with anger.

Clenching his jaw, Todd palmed the ball and moved in closer to the backboard. When he was in the circle, he practiced a series of left- and right-handed hook shots. Breathing hard, Todd retrieved the ball and dribbled it. His adrenaline coursing through his veins, he moved back to the free throw line. Squinting in concentration, he threw the ball smoothly into the basket.

Well, at least my game is on, Todd thought ironically as he caught the ball again. Wiping off his forehead with the back of his arm, he dribbled the ball slowly and headed to the sidelines. He took long, deep breaths to slow down his heart rate. Todd grabbed his towel from the bench and patted his face dry.

Wrapping the towel around his shoulders, Todd sat down to catch his breath. He slumped down on the bench, feeling dejected. Even though he had put himself through a drill that would make the coach proud, he didn't feel any better. He couldn't stop thinking about Elizabeth and Devon.

Todd stared across the court, wondering what Elizabeth was doing at that moment. She was probably at the *Oracle* office, working late to meet the upcoming weekly deadline. In the old days he would have swung by to pick her up and taken her out for a bite to eat. *Will she be doing that now with Devon instead?* Todd wondered.

Shaking his head hard, Todd grabbed his basketball and stood up. Sitting around feeling sorry for himself wasn't going to get him anywhere. He tucked the ball under his arm and headed for the locker room.

Half an hour later Todd walked out of the boys' locker room, his gym bag slung over his shoulder.

As he crossed the court he found his spirits had risen considerably. He had stretched and taken a cold shower. Apparently his workout had helped a bit after all. His muscles were pleasantly tired, and he felt as if he had accomplished something.

Shifting the weight of his gym bag, Todd pushed open the stadium door and swung into the hallway. But then he hesitated. If he continued in this direction, he would pass by the *Oracle* office. The last thing he wanted was to bump into Elizabeth and Devon acting all lovey-dovey together. Todd turned around quickly and went back in the opposite direction. His footsteps echoing in the empty stadium, he crossed the waxed floor of the gym and exited out the back.

It was clear and cool outside, and the crisp air felt good after his rigorous workout. The sun was just beginning to set, casting a rosy glow along the horizon. Todd took long, deep breaths, enjoying the feel of the fresh air in his lungs.

Todd headed around the building, whistling softly. As he made his way across the sprawling front lawn he gave himself a mental lecture. *Forget Elizabeth and Devon,* he told himself sternly. *You have to start thinking of yourself.*

Suddenly he saw a familiar figure on the front steps of school. Courtney Kane was sitting alone against a railing, her legs curled elegantly on the white steps.

Todd felt his heartbeat accelerate at the sight of

her. Courtney looked fresh and lovely. She was wearing a pair of light cotton pants and a delicate white blouse with tiny pearl buttons. Her thick chestnut hair was pulled back in a loose ponytail at the nape of her neck.

Feeling oddly nervous, Todd walked up the steps to join her.

Courtney smiled coyly when she saw him. "Hi, Todd," she said softly.

"Hey," Todd responded, sitting down on the steps next to her. He felt a bit hesitant. This was the first time he and Courtney had really spoken since their disastrous breakup. She didn't seem to be angry now, but he wasn't sure if she wanted his company.

Courtney shifted around to face him. "So what are you up to these days?" she asked.

Todd shrugged. "Nothing much," he responded gruffly. *Having my heart broken,* he thought. He scowled and looked down, scraping at the corner of the step with the bottom of his tennis shoe. Then he forced the depressing thought away. Shaking his head slightly, he turned his attention back to Courtney. "Are you waiting for someone?" he asked.

Courtney smoothed back a loose strand of hair. "I told Jessica I'd pick her up from cheerleading practice," she explained. "We're going to swing by Lila's and go for a slice of pizza."

Todd frowned. "Isn't Jessica kind of late?" he

asked. "Cheerleading practice should have been over about half an hour ago."

Courtney shrugged. "You know Jessica. She never—"

"Wears a watch." Todd finished the sentence with her, and they both laughed.

Todd looked away, feeling unexpectedly moved. It was the first time he had laughed since Elizabeth started seeing Devon. He felt lighter than he had in days.

Suddenly he saw Elizabeth walking across the lawn toward her car. He blinked, wondering if his mind were playing tricks on him. But there she was, walking slowly, her books tucked under her arms like usual.

What is she doing here? he wondered. *Why isn't she at the* Oracle *office?*

As if she sensed his eyes on her, Elizabeth turned and looked up at them, a slightly forlorn expression on her face. For a split second Todd felt as if he had been caught. *That's ridiculous,* he told himself sternly. Elizabeth was the one who cut him loose. He was free to talk to whomever he wanted.

Elizabeth stopped at the bottom of the steps, frowning. Then she dug a hand into her pocket and slid something onto her finger. Lifting her hand in the air, she gave Todd a small wave. Todd could see the sterling silver ring he had given her shining in the waning afternoon light.

Hugging her books tight to her chest, Elizabeth turned and walked away.

Todd felt his pulse pick up. Elizabeth was giving him a message. She wanted him after all!

But just as quickly his hope turned to anger. It had taken him talking to Courtney for Elizabeth to put that ring on. She had shown no interest in Todd until she saw him with another girl.

Todd's eyes narrowed angrily. This time Elizabeth had gone too far. He had been completely understanding until now. Todd had forgiven Elizabeth despite the fact that she had started seeing another guy behind his back. But this was too much. Todd wasn't some kind of toy to be played with. If Elizabeth didn't appreciate him for himself, then she wasn't worth it.

Todd turned back to Courtney and gave her an intimate smile. "Maybe we should just forget Lila and Jessica and go for that pizza ourselves. I seem to remember mushroom-and-pepperoni pie being your favorite. . . ."

"Success," Jessica whispered, an evil smile on her face. She watched in satisfaction as Todd and Courtney headed across the lawn to the parking lot. Her psychological maneuver had worked perfectly. She had been sure that "Elizabeth's" ring gesture would make Todd angry and send him right into the arms of another girl.

Smiling, Jessica transformed herself back to normal. She unfastened the top button of Elizabeth's conservative button-down shirt and shook her hair free of its clip. Then she put her books back into her backpack and swung it over her shoulder. And she removed the ring that Todd had given Elizabeth.

Just before Todd and Courtney turned the corner to the parking lot, Courtney glanced back over her shoulder. Her smoky eyes sparkling, Courtney flashed Jessica a big smile. Jessica smiled back, giving her a thumbs-up signal.

Maybe her afternoon with Devon hadn't gone as well as planned, but at least she had planted the idea that Elizabeth couldn't be trusted. And Todd was unwittingly playing into her hands. Now all she had to do was figure out what it would take to impress Devon once and for all. But first she had other things to attend to.

Jessica grinned devilishly and practically skipped toward Lila's car, which was parked behind the school. Lila was waiting for Jessica to help her put the final touches on her plot to get back at Elizabeth. It was time to show her sister what it felt like to see her true love with another girl.

"Do you remember the night we crashed my father's office party?" Todd asked, his coffee-colored eyes twinkling brightly.

Courtney laughed. "How could I forget?"

Courtney and Todd were sitting on the same side of a booth at Guido's Pizza Parlor. A large pepperoni-and-mushroom pizza sat in the middle of the table, along with a loaf of fresh garlic bread and a big pitcher of ice water. Courtney was having a great time. The food was delicious, and she and Todd had been talking nonstop for the past hour, reminiscing about the times they had shared together.

Courtney smiled to herself as she remembered the infamous event that Todd had brought up. She and Todd had snuck into the office building of Varitronics one night. Even though Courtney's father was a vice president of the company, she had never been inside the building, and she had asked Todd to give her a late night tour. She had actually just wanted an excuse to get him alone.

But her plan had totally backfired. Instead of finding themselves alone, they had walked right into the middle of an executive black-tie affair. Todd's father had been steaming mad. "I thought your father was going to explode," Courtney remarked. She reached for her diet Coke and took a sip through the straw.

Todd shook his head ruefully. "I don't think he's gotten over it yet." Todd picked up the pizza cutter and sliced two triangles of pizza from the serving dish. "Now every time he has a party, he's sure to warn me first." He placed one piece of pizza on Courtney's plate and the other on his own.

Courtney's blue eyes widened. "Is that true?" she asked.

Todd nodded, reaching for a piece of garlic

bread. "In fact, it's kind of become a family joke. Whenever he's planning an office affair, he sends me an invitation too. But he always writes 'you are not invited' on it."

Courtney giggled. Todd's family had always been a lot of fun. Mr. and Mrs. Wilkins were so playful that they seemed almost as young as the kids. Courtney picked up her soda, feeling wistful. She was surprised to find how many positive memories she had of her relationship with Todd. She was glad he'd finally decided to dump that boring old Elizabeth and get on with his life.

Todd turned to face her. "But you know, my parents really liked you," he said. He wiped the crumbs from his garlic bread off the table into his palm and brushed them off onto his plate.

Courtney lowered her eyelashes, feeling suddenly vulnerable. "They did?" she asked quietly. Todd's parents had been extremely friendly to her, but she hadn't been sure if their motives were genuine. Guys often wanted to date her because of her wealth and connections. She had thought Mr. Wilkins was encouraging their relationship because her father was a VIP in his company.

"Of course they liked you," Todd reassured her. Shifting closer to her, he caught her eyes with his. "After all, who could possibly resist somebody who's intelligent, cultivated—and breathtakingly beautiful?"

Courtney's face flushed at Todd's unexpected flattery, and she felt her heart flutter under the intensity of his gaze. Suddenly she remembered why she had had such a crush on Todd. He was everything she wanted in a guy—handsome, athletic, and a lot of fun. Her mind was less on Jessica's plan now than on feeling Todd's lips on hers again.

Blinking, Courtney drew back, trying to break the spell. If she could, she would lean over and kiss him right now. But she had to wait for the signal. Jessica had helped Courtney snag Todd again, so Courtney couldn't let Jessica down. She bit her lower lip in frustration. She could taste Todd's kisses already.

A few minutes later Jessica peeked into the door of Guido's Pizza Parlor. Lila had taken her home so she could change back into her own clothes. Now she was wearing a black cotton minidress and funky brown leather sandals. A big silver pendant hung around her neck. Jessica felt much better now. Elizabeth's beige pants and stiff cotton shirt had been completely constricting.

Lila had dropped her off and told her to call her on the cell phone when she was done with her scheme. Jessica scanned the crowded room quickly, looking for Courtney and Todd. She caught sight of them sitting on the same side of a big booth in front. They were leaning close together, talking eagerly. Smiling in satisfaction, Jessica quickly ducked back out the door.

Digging into her purse for change, she slipped into the phone booth outside the pizza parlor. She picked up the receiver and dropped a quarter into the slot. Her heart was beating quickly in her chest as she dialed the number of the *Oracle* office.

"Hello. Can I help you?" a cheerful male voice responded. Jessica recognized the voice as belonging to Mr. Collins, the twins' favorite English teacher and the faculty adviser of the newspaper.

Jessica put her hand on the receiver to block out the street noise and leaned in close to the phone. "Hi, Mr. Collins, it's Jessica Wakefield. Is Elizabeth there?"

"Hi, Jessica," Mr. Collins responded, his tone friendly. "If you hold on just a minute, I'll get her for you."

A few minutes later Elizabeth answered the phone, slightly out of breath.

"Hi, Liz, it's me," Jessica said. Cradling the receiver in the crook of her neck, she leaned back against the glass and crossed her legs at the ankle.

"Hey! How did your study session go?" Elizabeth asked.

Jessica gripped the phone tightly and tried to keep the anger over her afternoon with Devon out of her voice. "It was great," she lied. "Devon's so intelligent. We had a wonderful time."

"That's . . . great," Elizabeth said slowly. There was an edge in her voice, and Jessica smiled. She'd love to continue making Elizabeth squirm over thoughts of Jessica and Devon, but she had other things to attend to.

"So listen, I need you to do me a huge favor," Jessica said. "I left my English homework in my locker. Do you think you could get it for me?"

"Sure, no problem," Elizabeth responded quickly. "What's your combination again?"

"Twenty-five, twenty-two, three," Jessica supplied, shifting the receiver to her other ear. "My English assignment is in a blue folder. It should be lying right on top of my books."

Just then a car honked from the street.

"Hey, where are you?" Elizabeth asked.

"I'm at Guido's Pizza Parlor," Jessica explained. "I came over with Lila, but she had to go home. Why don't you stop by when you're finished so we can get something to eat?" Jessica held her breath as she waited for her sister's response.

"Well, actually I'm done now, but I was thinking of seeing what Devon was up to. Did he say where he was going after the library?" Elizabeth asked.

Jessica frowned, letting out her breath in a rush.

"Elizabeth, if you want to make up for what you did, you could at least spend a little bit of time with me," Jessica said in a petulant tone. She knew her sister would cave at her words. Guilt always got to Elizabeth. "You can see Devon tomorrow," she added.

"You're right," Elizabeth agreed. "I'll be there in fifteen minutes."

Jessica smiled into the phone. "I'll be waiting for you," she said.

Chapter 8

"And then we turned Monsieur Arnaud's desk upside down," Courtney said, waving an elegant hand in the air as she spoke. "And we placed all his papers on the underside of the desk."

Todd burst out laughing. Courtney had been regaling him for the past hour with stories about Lovett Academy. It was a very old, sober prep school, and apparently Courtney and her friends liked to stir things up a bit.

Courtney giggled. "You should have seen the look on his face." She made a stern face and put on an exaggerated French accent. "I weell not have zees! Dis eez entirely unazzeptable!"

Todd couldn't help smiling at Courtney's comic imitation. "So what did the teacher do?" he asked. He picked up the pitcher of ice water and filled up their glasses.

Courtney grinned. "Actually he handled it pretty well," she said, shifting in her seat and curling her legs under her. "He made us turn our desks upside down as well."

Todd whistled under his breath. "I would've loved to see that." He took a long gulp of water.

Courtney nodded. "It wasn't too easy for us to take notes that day," she said.

Todd shook his head, amused by the image. "I can imagine."

He sat back comfortably in the booth, surprised at what a terrific time he was having with Courtney. It was a huge relief to be enjoying himself after feeling so heavy and miserable all week.

Just then the waiter arrived at their table. Todd didn't know his name, but he recognized him as a sophomore from Sweet Valley High. He had sandy blond hair and light blue eyes. "Did you want anything else?" he asked, picking up their dishes and setting them on his tray.

"No, thanks," Courtney said with a small shake of her head. "But everything was delicious." She gave the waiter a charming smile, which accentuated the cleft in her chin.

"Uh . . . uh . . . great," the guy responded, stuttering slightly. He knocked over an empty glass on the table and quickly righted it. "Oh, sorry," he muttered. Clearly embarrassed, he turned and hurried away.

"Wow, I'm impressed," Todd said after the

116

waiter had left. "One smile from you and that guy was reduced to nothing."

Courtney blushed. "Todd, stop flattering me!" she protested. But she was clearly pleased at the remark, and the rosy glow to her cheeks only served to enhance her beauty.

Todd looked at her in admiration. Now he remembered why they had gone out in the first place. They had had a lot of fun together in the short time they dated. Not to mention the fact that Courtney was absolutely gorgeous.

"Well, the waiter's not the only guy you've got power over," Todd remarked. Draping an arm around her shoulders, he drew her closer to him.

"Mmm," she murmured, snuggling up to him. She was so close that Todd could smell the sweet scent of her perfume. He cupped her chin in his hand and turned her face to his. Courtney looked deep into his eyes, and Todd's heart skipped a beat. Taking a deep breath, he leaned in to kiss her.

Suddenly a phone jangled, and they both jumped.

Todd looked around, bewildered. "Where did that come from?"

"Sorry. It's mine," Courtney said. Opening up her big black leather bag, she drew out a cellular phone. It rang again in her hand. Courtney gave an exasperated sigh. "These things are more annoying than useful," she remarked. "Why don't we just turn this off?"

117

Courtney clicked off the phone without answering the call. Pushing the antenna back in, she shoved the phone back in her bag and zipped it shut.

Todd shrugged. "Fine by me," he agreed, drawing her closer to him again. "Then I can have you all to myself."

Courtney smiled in appreciation. Turning to face him, she leaned in and kissed him on the cheek. And lightly on the lips. Todd shivered with pleasure and returned her kiss. Soon they were exchanging a real, long embrace.

Todd knew everyone in the place was watching. But for once he didn't care.

Elizabeth swung the twins' Jeep onto Valley Crest Road, humming softly to herself. It was a lovely evening. The sky was a cobalt blue, and streaks of pink and orange hovered above the horizon. The sweet smell of honeysuckle scented the cool air.

Elizabeth switched on the radio and flipped the knob, stopping at a soft rock station. She was disappointed that she wouldn't be able to see Devon that evening, but she was glad to get a chance to spend some quality time with her sister. After all, Jessica was right. Elizabeth *did* owe her. Now they could have their sisters' night out after all.

Singing along with the music, Elizabeth coasted down the street. She felt more peaceful than she had in days. Things were working out with Devon for the moment, and they were going to be hanging out a lot now that he'd decided to compete in the science fair.

Elizabeth just hoped that Jessica didn't think having Devon tutoring her would somehow bring the two of them together. Jessica had come up with stranger plans than that before. Elizabeth decided that she'd ask her sister about the tutoring session again over dinner and gauge her response for signs of guilt. Even though she knew Devon wasn't interested in Jessica and was only trying to be helpful, Elizabeth couldn't be so sure about her sister's motives.

Now if I could only figure out what to do about Todd, Elizabeth thought as she turned into the parking lot of Guido's Pizza Parlor. She couldn't stand the idea of him sitting alone at home, pining away for her. And she missed him.

Elizabeth pulled the Jeep into a spot, pushing the disturbing thought away. She was sure that she and Todd could be friends eventually. For now she had to take things one step at a time. And at the moment she was going to patch up her relationship with Jessica.

Unbuckling her seat belt with her left hand, Elizabeth leaned over and grabbed her backpack. She jumped out of the Jeep and shut the door behind her, swinging her backpack over her shoulder. Then she walked quickly across the crowded lot.

Elizabeth pulled open the door of the restaurant and stepped inside. The smell of freshly baked pizza wafted through the air, and she felt her stomach growl in hunger. Stepping through the line that had formed at the door, Elizabeth glanced around the room for her twin.

The popular hangout was hopping. The wooden booths were crammed with students sharing Guido's famous pizza pies and chattering loudly. The artificial waterfall in the back of the restaurant added a low roaring sound to the din of the restaurant.

Elizabeth recognized a few members of the cheerleading squad sitting at a booth near the window, but she didn't see her sister among them. Squinting, she glanced at the bar at the far end of the room. Jessica wasn't there either. Elizabeth frowned, wondering where her sister was. Jessica had said that she was already at the restaurant.

Maybe she's at one of the tables in back, Elizabeth thought. Shrugging, she made her way through the crowd at the door.

Suddenly she stood stock-still. Todd was sitting in a booth right in front. And Courtney Kane was wrapped in his arms, kissing him passionately. Elizabeth stared, shocked at their public display of affection.

A searing pain ripped through Elizabeth's heart. Her Todd. With Courtney Kane—again! Her stomach coiled in disgust, and she was hit with an overwhelming sense of possessiveness. *No, no, no!* she thought, shaking her head frantically. *It's not possible*. But she couldn't deny the horrible sight right in front of her. Hot tears rushed to her eyes, and she blinked them back rapidly.

All thoughts of Jessica forgotten, Elizabeth turned and raced out of the pizza parlor.

"See you later, Liz," Jessica said out loud, watching in satisfaction as Elizabeth fled from the restaurant. A tiny smile twitched at the corner of her lips.

Jessica was sitting at a corner booth in back, calmly drinking a glass of soda. A plate of nachos and salsa sat in front of her. She reached for a chip and dipped it in the bowl of sauce.

Elizabeth was usually superresponsible, reflected Jessica, crunching into her chip. It wasn't like her to shirk her responsibilities. But Elizabeth had been so upset at the sight of Todd and Courtney that she hadn't even bothered to find Jessica and hand over her homework. Her sister was obviously devastated.

For a moment Jessica felt a sharp twinge of guilt. Elizabeth really looked upset. She'd had tears in her eyes, and the expression on her face was one of total horror. Jessica frowned, drumming her fingers on the table in front of her. Maybe she had gone too far this time.

But then Jessica pushed her guilty feelings away. Stuffing a handful of chips in her mouth, she forced herself to recall how Elizabeth had betrayed her. She thought again of how Elizabeth had stolen Devon. Her own sister had thought nothing of taking away the guy Jessica was completely in love with. Instead of putting in a good word for Jessica in chemistry class, Elizabeth had used her own charms to win Devon's affection. And then she had set Jessica up at the Box Tree Café to make a total fool out of her.

Jessica crunched into her nachos angrily as she remembered Devon's harsh words to her. "I could easily use you, Jessica," he had said bitterly. "And then throw you away."

Jessica squeezed her eyes tight, the humiliating moment returning to her in full force. *No,* she thought, *I have no reason to feel guilty. Elizabeth is getting exactly what she deserves.*

Elizabeth sped along the coastal highway, hot tears streaming down her face. The night was cool, and the deep blue ocean sparkled to her right. Elizabeth unrolled her window and turned her face to the wind, letting the brisk air whip back her hair. Holding the steering wheel in her left hand, she rubbed her wet eyes with the back of her sleeve.

Todd and Courtney Kane! Another tear came to her eye, and Elizabeth brushed it angrily away. She thought back to the time Todd went out with Courtney. He told Elizabeth afterward that

Courtney had meant nothing to him. "I was just trying to make you jealous," he had said. But obviously that was a lie.

Elizabeth frowned. *Was it* all *a lie?* she wondered. *Was our entire relationship a lie?* She sniffed, feeling hurt and bewildered. She couldn't believe that Todd could rebound so fast. *It didn't take him long to replace me,* Elizabeth thought. *Like one day.* She shook her head, wondering if she had meant anything to him in the first place.

Wind whipped through her hair, and Elizabeth took long, deep breaths of the salty sea air, trying to settle her nerves. She glanced at the ocean to the right, lulled by the steady roar of the waves. A lone seagull flew across the sea, cutting an arcing pattern over the water.

Feeling somewhat calmer, Elizabeth cut her speed. She took the next exit ramp and turned off the coastal highway, then swung the Jeep around and got back on the highway leading in the other direction.

Elizabeth frowned in confusion as she headed back to Sweet Valley. Why was she having such a strong reaction to seeing Todd with another girl? Wasn't that what she had wanted all along? Did this mean that she was still in love with Todd?

Sighing, Elizabeth leaned her head back against the headrest. This whole situation was too confusing. One minute she thought she was in love with Devon, and the next she thought she still loved

Todd. *Is it possible to be in love with two people at once?* she wondered.

As Elizabeth entered the town of Sweet Valley she forced herself to calm down and look at the situation rationally. Before she went home, she decided, she had to work out her feelings. She had to figure out what was making her respond so irrationally to seeing Todd and Courtney together.

Driving in no particular direction, Elizabeth steered the Jeep along the tiny, winding roads of the quiet town. The sky was dark now, and the streets were almost deserted. Elizabeth knew most people were inside having dinner with their families. But Elizabeth just wanted to be alone.

She found herself at the little park where she and Todd had shared their first kiss. Feeling nostalgic, Elizabeth slowed down to a stop. She remembered how they had embraced for the first time under the big oak tree. The entire world had turned upside down since then.

Propping her knees up on the dashboard, Elizabeth started to recall all the special times she and Todd had shared. They'd been through so much together, from him moving away to her brief fling with his best friend, Ken Matthews, to their many silly breakups. How could things shift so quickly?

Suddenly everything became clear, and Elizabeth sat up straight in her seat. It was *normal* for her to be upset by seeing Todd with another girl. After all, she and Todd had practically shared a lifetime together. Of course it hurt to see him with someone else.

This is how Todd must have felt seeing me with Devon, she thought, turning the key in the ignition. He must have been just as confused as she was now. And he must have felt equally hurt and betrayed.

Elizabeth coasted down the street, feeling much more peaceful than she had an hour ago. If she wanted to move on, she had to let Todd do the same. If she were really generous about it, then she'd be happy for him.

In fact, Elizabeth realized, it was the perfect solution. If she could get Todd excited about his new relationship, then she would be free to pursue hers as well. It was simple. She just had to push aside her own feelings of hurt and jealousy.

Elizabeth turned onto Valley Crest Drive and headed back home, feeling determined to rise above the situation. She was going to show Todd just how much she really did care for him—by letting him go completely.

"What?" Jessica exclaimed in shock. "You're going to set your own boyfriend up with another girl?"

The twins were in Jessica's bedroom late Wednesday night, and Jessica couldn't believe her ears. She had been in a great mood until her sister came home. When Elizabeth had walked into her room smiling and cheerful, Jessica's spirits had instantly fallen. Apparently Elizabeth was perfectly fine about the situation with Todd and Courtney.

"Ex-boyfriend," Elizabeth corrected her.

"But—but—," Jessica stuttered, finding herself at a loss for words. She shut her mouth and sat down hard on the bed.

Elizabeth smiled as she took a seat at Jessica's desk. "I've made a mature decision," she explained. "I'm going to make sure this really works between Todd and Courtney. That way I'll be free to move on. And to stay friends with Todd in the process."

Jessica's eyes widened. "Are you saying you're going to coax Todd and Courtney along?" Shoving a pile of clothes on the floor, she tapped a foot in agitation.

Elizabeth nodded. "Exactly," she affirmed. "In fact, I should have thought of it sooner."

Jessica clenched her hand into a fist, feeling her chance at revenge slipping from her grasp. She stood up and faced her sister, holding a hand out in a pleading gesture. "Listen, Liz, you've got to think rationally about this."

Elizabeth smiled at her serenely. "I *am* thinking rationally," she countered. "I've decided to rise above my feelings, that's all."

Jessica shook her head. "What do you mean? This is completely irrational. Nobody sets her boyfriend up with another girl." Jessica held her hands up to her head, pacing along the carpet. "It's unheard of. It's crazy. It's sick."

126

Elizabeth looked amused. "You're being a little overdramatic, don't you think?"

Jessica clenched her jaw in frustration. Her sister was completely unshakable this evening. She didn't know what had come over her. Jessica knew her twin better than anybody, but suddenly Elizabeth was acting like a total stranger.

Jessica studied her sister. Elizabeth was sitting calmly in the chair, a tranquil expression on her face. She almost had an aura of peace about her. Jessica narrowed her eyes suspiciously. "What is this? Some kind of new zen thing?"

Elizabeth laughed and shrugged. "If you want to call it that."

Jessica opened her mouth to protest further, but then she shut it again. Obviously none of her arguments were going to work. Elizabeth had her mind set on encouraging Todd and Courtney's relationship, and nothing was going to make her reconsider.

Elizabeth stood up and stretched her arms above her head. "Well, I'm going to get ready for bed," she said with a yawn. "It's been a long day, and I want to think about my science project before going to sleep."

An alarm went off in Jessica's head, and she whipped around to face her sister. "What science project?" she asked quickly.

"Devon and I are going to compete in the science fair," Elizabeth explained. She took a few steps across the carpet, her eyes shining in excitement. "I'm surprised he didn't tell you about it at the library. Devon came up with a great idea. We're definitely going to win."

Jessica's heart sank. This was the last straw. If Elizabeth and Devon took part in the fair, they would be spending even more time together. And Jessica had pretty much killed her own chances of hanging out with Devon when she'd thrown that little tantrum this afternoon. Why did everything keep going wrong? "So what's the idea?" she asked with a frown.

Elizabeth's blue-green eyes twinkled mysteriously. "It's a secret," she said, a half smile on her lips. "I promised Devon I wouldn't talk about it."

Jessica rolled her eyes. "As if I'm going to steal it."

Elizabeth shrugged, pulling open the door leading to the bathroom adjoining the twins' rooms. "Well, good night," she said. "Sleep well."

"You too," Jessica grumbled.

Jessica plopped down onto the edge of the bed, feeling totally foiled. Not only had her plan backfired, but now Elizabeth and Devon were probably going to end up on an all-expenses-paid trip to San Francisco.

That was the clincher. In her mind's eye Jessica could see Elizabeth and Devon walking along the boardwalk hand in hand, the Pacific Ocean roaring in the distance. Jessica squeezed her hand into a tight fist. *She* was the one who should be Devon's partner in the fair. And *she* was the one who should be spending a romantic weekend with him in San Francisco.

Jessica fell back onto the covers, staring at the ceiling in despair. It seemed that no matter what she did, she only succeeding in bringing Devon and Elizabeth closer together. Not only was Todd safely out of the picture, but now Devon and Elizabeth were going to be spending all their time together working on their science project. Soon they would be frolicking together on the cobbled streets of the City by the Bay. The image made her stomach clench.

Banish the thought, Jessica commanded herself. She shook her head hard and sat up. There *had* to be a way to prevent Devon and Elizabeth from taking first prize at the fair. And there had to be a way to make Devon notice her again.

Jessica drummed her fingers along the edge of the bed, deep in thought. *Forget sexy miniskirts and seductive smiles,* she thought. If she'd learned one thing from her little encounter with Devon at the library today, it was that the way to Devon's heart was through his head. Jessica had to show him that she was just as talented in the sciences as Elizabeth.

The kernel of an idea formed in Jessica's head, and she sat up straighter. What better place to show off her talents than at the science fair? Jessica wasn't quite sure how she'd pull it off, but one thing was certain—everything was going to come to a head at the fair. Jessica leaned back on her elbows, the wheels of her mind turning. *Maybe things* will *work out in the end,* she thought with a tiny smile. *Maybe I'll get what I want after all.*

Chapter 9

"Ah! The mad scientist is hard at work," Elizabeth teased as she slipped into her seat next to Devon in chemistry class on Thursday morning.

Devon sat hunched over a yellow legal pad, scribbling furiously. His cheeks were flushed, and his hair was in disarray. He looked up and smiled at her. "I've almost got the formula," he said, his blue eyes shining. Then he quickly turned back to his work.

Elizabeth smiled in anticipation. Apparently Devon was just as excited about their project as she was. They had decided to put together a project on sound waves and their different frequencies. He had suggested the idea of making a dulcimer, a stringed instrument that was played with hammers. Then they would explain how each string was specially placed to produce a different frequency.

Devon muttered something under his breath

and tapped the eraser end of his pencil on the page. Elizabeth leaned over to see what he was doing. Her eyes widened as she took in the page he was working on. It was covered in complicated formulas, written at all angles.

Devon narrowed his eyes and studied his equation. Then he scribbled down a few more calculations. Chewing on the wood of the pencil, he cocked his head and examined the result. He reached for his pocket calculator and quickly punched in a few numbers. Holding up the calculator, he compared the two results.

"Shoot!" Devon exclaimed, ripping the page off the pad and crumpling it up. He threw the wad of paper in a pile in a corner, where it joined a number of other yellow balls.

Elizabeth smiled to herself. Devon really *was* acting like a mad scientist this morning. He was obviously too preoccupied to think about chemistry class. She would have to start their lab assignment herself. Elizabeth opened her book to the chapter on thermodynamics. Sitting back, she began reading through the section on energy and heat.

Fifteen minutes later Devon let out a quiet whoop of joy. "I've got it!" he exclaimed, his eyes shining with excitement. "Elizabeth, look!"

Elizabeth leaned over to see. On the bottom of the page, under all the equations and formulas, Devon had sketched a rectangular-shaped musical instrument. It was composed of a series of wires stretched across a diagonal line of cubes. A long hammer with a cork on the end of it was drawn in at the bottom.

Elizabeth sucked in her breath. "It's like a miniature harp!" she exclaimed in a loud whisper. She and Devon had decided to keep their idea secret until the day of the fair. They wanted it to be a surprise.

Devon nodded. "Exactly," he said, keeping his voice low. "The principle is pretty much the same except that we strike the strings instead of plucking them."

"So we hit the wires with the hammer to produce a tone?" Elizabeth asked.

"That's right," Devon said. "But the beauty of this is its complexity." He leaned in close and spoke in a soft voice. "The way strings produce different vibrations is complicated. When one of these strings is hit with the hammer, all different kinds of harmonies and tones are produced."

Elizabeth bit her lip in excitement. "I can't believe we're actually going to create a musical instrument!"

Devon held a finger up to his lips, a playful expression on his face. "Watch out. This is top secret, remember?"

Elizabeth clapped her hand to her mouth, looking around to make sure nobody had heard her. But the students around her were all hard at work on their lab assignments. She turned back to Devon with a grin. "Agent double-oh-eight, sworn to secrecy."

Devon smiled back. "Agent double-oh-seven, message received."

Elizabeth giggled. "So when do we start?"

Devon winked and spoke in a conspiratorial whisper. "Tonight. My place."

"Hey! Jessica! Wait up," Devon called. Jessica was hurrying toward the cafeteria, and Devon wanted to catch her so he could apologize for hurting her feelings at the library. He hated it when he spoke without thinking.

Jessica stopped and turned around slowly. "Hi, Devon!" she said, smiling pleasantly. Devon felt slightly relieved. She didn't look mad at all.

"Listen," he said, stuffing his hands in the pockets of his leather jacket. "I'm really sorry about what I said yesterday. I just—"

"No problem," Jessica said, patting him on the shoulder. "I didn't mean to blow up on you either. Why don't we pretend the whole thing never happened?"

Devon raised his eyebrows. He was surprised that Jessica could be so levelheaded and understanding. Maybe he didn't know her as well as he thought. "It's forgotten," he said with an easy smile.

"Great!" Jessica said. "I gotta go. I have a meeting with the cheerleaders, and they're lost without me. I'll see you later." With that, Jessica pushed through the cafeteria doors and disappeared into the crowd. Devon shook his head. That girl never stopped moving.

He sauntered into the cafeteria to join Elizabeth for lunch, his spirits high. He was glad Jessica wasn't mad at him. He didn't want Elizabeth to find out what a jerk he'd been to her sister. And he was glad he'd decided to take part in the science fair. He was really excited about their project. There was nothing he liked better than coming up with an idea and seeing it through. The science of sound was a new field to him, and he was looking forward to exploring it.

Suddenly Bruce Patman stepped into his path, blocking his way. "Hey, man, how are you doing?" Bruce asked.

"I'm all right," Devon responded evenly.

He shifted to the right, but Bruce moved as well. Devon sighed, feeling trapped. Bruce Patman was the kind of guy who turned him off completely. He gave Devon the impression of being a typical spoiled rich kid who was good-looking and knew it. Today he was wearing a pair of dark sunglasses, and a piece of grass hung out of the side of his mouth.

For some reason Bruce had made every attempt to become friends with Devon. He had offered to show him the coolest spots in Sweet Valley and to give him a tour of the hottest nightclubs in L.A. Bruce had thrown a big party Friday night, and he had made a point of mentioning it to Devon. Devon had politely refused all his invitations, but Bruce didn't seem to get the hint.

Bruce chewed on the blade of grass. "Some of my friends are having lunch over there," he said, pointing to a bunch of macho-looking seniors sitting at a table in the corner. All the guys had crew cuts and pumped-up torsos. Devon's stomach turned at the sight of them. "Do you wanna join us?"

Devon shifted uncomfortably. "Thanks, maybe another time," he said. He glanced around the lunchroom for Elizabeth.

"No problem," Bruce said with a wave of his hand. He turned the piece of grass in the corner of his mouth. "So, I heard you're an ace tennis player," he remarked.

Devon frowned. He couldn't imagine where Bruce had gotten that information. Devon had been a member of the tennis team at his old school in Connecticut, but he hadn't even set foot on a court since he'd been in Sweet Valley. Devon sighed. Despite the fact that he liked to keep a low profile, he seemed to attract a lot of attention.

But Devon didn't want to let his discomfort show. "I can hit the ball around," he responded with a shrug.

Bruce gave him a cool smile. "Well, I'm the star of the SVH tennis team," he boasted. "I could use a partner of my caliber. Why don't you think about joining the team?"

Devon grimaced. He liked to play tennis to work off steam, and he could think of nothing less relaxing than being Bruce's partner on the team. Shifting his weight, he pushed a lock of hair off his forehead. "I appreciate the thought," Devon said politely, "but I'm kind of easing into things right now."

Bruce grinned. "Well, we could just go bat the ball around one day after school."

Devon nodded. "Yeah," he responded vaguely. "Let's do that." He tapped a foot impatiently on the ground. "Listen, I'm meeting somebody, and I'm going to be late. If you don't mind—"

But Bruce didn't budge. "Oh, one more thing. It's guys' night out on Saturday night at my place. Typical male-bonding stuff—music, pool, poker." He gave Devon a conspiratorial wink. "Thought you might be interested."

"Thanks, but I don't think so," Devon said.

"No chicks," Bruce added with a snicker.

Devon shook his head, getting impatient. "It's really not my scene."

"But—," Bruce protested.

"Look, Bruce, the answer is no," Devon said firmly. Then he turned and walked away. As he made his way across the cafeteria he could feel Bruce's furious eyes boring a hole in his back.

Jessica sat alone at her lab table on Thursday afternoon in chemistry class, wondering where

Bruce was. Usually she would have been thrilled if he didn't show up for class, but today she needed him to put her plan in motion.

She had been so tempted to blurt out her plans to Devon before lunch today, she'd had to force herself to walk away from him so she wouldn't let the news out. She couldn't tell anyone she wanted to sign up for the science fair until Bruce agreed. No use in ruining her reputation unless she was going to see the plan through to the end.

Jessica drummed her fingers on the tabletop. Around her, students were huddled in groups working on their lab assignments. Jessica sighed impatiently. Leaning over, she reached into her bag and pulled out a thick blue nail file. She laid a hand flat on her chemistry book and began shaping her nails.

"Do you need some help?" Mr. Russo asked, approaching from behind.

Jessica jumped. Making a fist around her nail file to hide it, she turned and gave him her most charming smile. "Oh, no, thanks, Mr. Russo," she said in a sugary sweet voice. "I was just getting started." She quickly opened her book and flipped to the day's lesson.

Mr. Russo smiled back. "Well, let me know if you have any problems," he said.

Jessica breathed a sigh of relief as he moved down the aisle. Frowning, she skimmed the chapter covering thermodynamic processes. Their lab assignment was to create a calorimeter that measured the amount of heat released from a piece of cooling metal.

Following the instructions in her lab manual, Jessica gathered together the supplies for the day's lesson. When she was ready to begin, she turned and consulted her book. The first step was to heat up a piece of metal. With a pair of tongs she picked up a square of metal from the supply basket and laid it carefully in the bottom of a beaker. Then she flicked on the Bunsen burner and set the beaker on a piece of wire mesh on top of the burner.

Just then Bruce stormed into the room, clearly in a foul mood.

"Hi, Bruce," Jessica said, giving him a big smile as he took his seat next to her.

"Wakefield," he bit out shortly. He threw his backpack on the ground and sat down on his stool.

Jessica rolled her eyes and turned back to her work. Bruce was obviously his usual obnoxious self today. Following the diagram in the lab manual, she filled up a plastic foam cup with water from the sink. Using a pair of tongs, she plucked out the hot piece of metal from the beaker on the Bunsen burner and dropped it in the water. Then she inserted a thermometer into the cup and put on the lid.

"This is a foam cup calorimeter," she explained to Bruce. "The temperature change in the water is supposed to measure the amount of heat released from the piece of metal."

Jessica waved her hand to indicate the experiment and knocked over the cup in the process. "Darn it!" she exclaimed, jumping off her stool as a stream of water spilled over the side of the table. She grabbed a cloth and quickly mopped up the mess.

"Nice going, Einstein." Bruce snorted.

Jessica could feel her anger rising. Bruce had a lot of nerve criticizing her when he hadn't even bothered to show up for class on time. At least she was *trying* to perform the experiment.

But Jessica bit back a terse response. She couldn't alienate Bruce today. She needed him for the moment. When she had cleaned everything up, she turned to him with a friendly smile. "Well, should we try it again?" she asked.

"I guess so," Bruce grumbled.

As soon as the experiment was functioning, Jessica sat back and crossed her legs. "You know, I was thinking. Since we're such a good lab team, why don't we enter the science fair on Saturday?"

Bruce looked at her like she was out of her mind. "Since when are you turning into a geek?" he asked.

Jessica sighed, running a finger through her hair. "Bruce, believe me, I've got my reasons," she said.

"I sure hope so," Bruce scoffed. "If not, we're going to have to send you to the loony bin." He grinned, obviously finding himself amusing.

Jessica squeezed her eyes shut, feeling desperate. The science fair was her last chance to get Devon back. If she and Bruce came up with a really fabulous project, they would ruin Elizabeth and Devon's chance at winning. And Devon would fall in love with Jessica again. He would realize that he had misjudged her, and he would beg her for another chance. Then Elizabeth would know exactly how it felt to lose Devon.

"Bruce, *please* be my partner in the fair," she pleaded with him.

"What's in it for me?" Bruce asked.

"I'll do all your chemistry homework for the rest of the semester," Jessica offered quickly.

Bruce laughed. "What?" he said. "If you don't mind, I'd like to graduate this year."

"Very funny," Jessica retorted, tapping her index finger on the table. "OK, how about if I round up the cheerleaders to cheer at your next tennis tournament?" she proposed.

Bruce snickered. "Nice offer, but I think all those legs might distract me from my game."

Jessica heaved a sigh. "Fine," she said. "Then I'll spend the day scrubbing your mansion." Jessica groaned inside at the thought of it. There was nothing she hated more than cleaning. For a moment she wondered if she really were losing her mind.

Bruce looked at her carefully. "Wow, you must *really* be desperate," he remarked.

"So you'll do it?" Jessica asked hopefully.

But Bruce shook his head. "It's a nice offer and everything, but we've already got a full staff to take care of the premises."

Jessica pouted and slumped down on the table, fresh out of ideas.

"Look, Jessica, I don't know what's gotten into you," Bruce said. "Science fairs are for nerds like that walking test tube Devon."

Jessica tilted her head. "You don't like him?"

Bruce's eyes flashed angrily. "No, I don't like him at all. That guy has got to be put in his place. He thinks he's better than the rest of us."

Jessica nodded and sat up straight. "That's exactly why we've got to take part in this fair," she explained excitedly. "To bring him down to size."

"What do you mean?" Bruce asked, his interest clearly piqued.

Jessica leaned in close. "Apparently Devon is some sort of science genius. He's sure to win the fair. And that's just going to make his ego sky-rocket." Jessica sighed. "And his popularity."

Bruce's eyes narrowed in thought. Then he nodded slowly. "All right, you're on, Wakefield. Come over to my place tonight, and we'll come up with something."

Chapter 10

"A volcano?" Jessica exclaimed, staring at Bruce in horror. "You want to make a *volcano?*" It was Friday evening, and Jessica and Bruce were in the rec room of the Patman mansion, trying to come up with an idea for their science project.

The Patmans' entertainment room was a miniature world unto itself. There was a full-size pool table, a complete sound system, and a big screen onto which movies could be projected. Thick, burnt orange carpeting covered the floor, and solid wooden panels lined the walls. A pair of plush sofas sat next to the movie projector.

Bruce put his hands on his hips and glared at her. "You got any better ideas?" he asked.

Jessica thought quickly. She and Bruce had been working steadily for two days, but they couldn't seem to get anything to run properly. They had tried out a number of projects, including a miniature solar car and a model submarine, but all of them failed. Despite the expensive equipment that Bruce bought, everything kept short-circuiting and exploding. "How about a piano cocktail?" she suggested finally.

"A what?" Bruce asked.

"It's a miniature piano," Jessica explained. "I saw it in a movie once. When you play the keys, the piano makes a cocktail."

Bruce's eyes looked like they were going to pop out of his head. "Jessica, this isn't a movie. This is real life. You think we can just whip up a piano that makes drinks in one night?" Bruce leaned back against the pool table, shaking his head in disgust. "Besides, that's the stupidest idea I've ever heard of."

Jessica scowled. "It's better than a *volcano*," she said.

"Look, we have no choice," Bruce insisted. "Either we make a volcano or we give up."

"Fine," Jessica agreed, sinking down into an armchair with a sigh. "A volcano it is."

"Hey, partner," Devon said softly as he opened the door for Elizabeth on Friday evening. He had invited her over to his place so they could put the finishing touches on their project.

"Hi," Elizabeth responded with a smile, feeling her heart flutter at the sight of him. Devon was dressed casually in a pair of faded jeans and a white T-shirt that highlighted his lean torso and his strong arms. He was barefoot, and a turquoise bandanna was tied around his head.

Devon took Elizabeth's hand and led her down the hall. "I think we're all set," he said, his voice animated. "I got all the supplies we need this afternoon."

Elizabeth grinned. "I was afraid you might have already finished before I got here."

Devon pretended to be insulted. "Are you kidding? I'd never do that. We're a team."

Resting his hand lightly on the small of her back, he ushered her into the den. In just a few days they had managed to transform the cozy room into a work shed. A white drop cloth covered the floor, and different-size milk crates were scattered about the room. A tool kit sat open on the coffee table, revealing a set of screwdrivers and big coils of wire. Devon had put together a paint center in the corner, complete with cans of paint, a number of brushes, and a big jar of polyurethane gloss.

Elizabeth stepped gingerly into the room, carefully avoiding the tools on the floor. The skeleton of their dulcimer was laid out on a low wooden bench. Turning over a milk crate, Elizabeth sat down in front of it and examined their work.

Devon and Elizabeth had constructed the frame the day before out of an old cigar box. In order to create a support for the strings, they had pounded in two rows of small nails on the outside edges of the rectangular box. Twisting thin brass wires around the nails on one end, they had drawn them over the box to the adjoining nails on the other side. Now nine horizontal wire rows stretched across the top of the box.

Devon pulled up a milk crate and took a seat next to her. "So what do you think?" he asked.

Elizabeth smiled excitedly. "It looks good so far, though it's hard to believe that this is actually going to make music."

Devon's expression grew thoughtful. "I was thinking we could give it to Nan if it works. She used to play the piano and the cello when she was a kid. I know it's something she misses." He turned to her, a quizzical look on his face. "What do you think?"

"Devon, that's a wonderful idea," Elizabeth said softly. "That way you could give her something in return for all that she's done for you." Elizabeth had met Nan the night before and had liked her right away. Nan was warm and welcoming. She had invited Elizabeth to dinner and had stayed up talking to them while they worked. She and Devon seemed to be very close.

Devon nodded, stretching his long legs out in front of him. "That's what I was thinking."

"Hey, where is Nan, by the way?" Elizabeth asked.

"She's at a PTA dinner—which means we're all alone," Devon said with a mischievous grin. Wrapping his arm around her waist, he leaned in for a searing kiss. A tingling sensation traveled all the way down Elizabeth's body to the tips of her toes. Closing her eyes, she returned the kiss with the same ardor.

Finally Elizabeth pulled back breathlessly. "At this rate we're never going to get finished," she said.

Devon shook his head. "You're right," he agreed with a laugh. "But I'm not used to having such an enticing lab partner." He smiled at her, but then his face turned serious as he stared into her eyes. Leaning forward, he kissed her softly on the lips.

"Dev-on!" Elizabeth exclaimed when they separated.

"Oh, sorry, sorry," Devon said, holding his hands up in mock surrender. "Maybe you should put a paper bag over your head."

Elizabeth giggled. "Now, come on," she reprimanded him. "We've got a lot of work to do."

"OK, OK, let's get down to business." Devon studied the cigar box for a moment. "What we've got to do is create a sort of scale by adding tension to the wires."

Sorting through the supplies on the coffee table, Devon picked out a long, square measuring rod. He carefully inserted it under the strings, pushing it all the way to the left side of the box until it was taut. Leaning back on his heels, he narrowed his eyes in thought. "Now we've got to insert some kind of small cubes on a slant to produce different tones." Devon frowned suddenly. "Shoot," he muttered. "I forgot about the cubes."

"Don't worry, we'll come up with something," Elizabeth reassured him, rummaging through the tool kit. But all she found were assorted screws and nails. Shutting the lid, she glanced around the room. Her eyes lit on a board game sitting underneath the TV in the corner, and she hopped up quickly.

"Jackpot!" Elizabeth exclaimed as she pulled open the lid of the game. Sitting on top of the folded-up board was a pile of dice and a miniature hourglass.

"Would dice work?" she asked, holding up a handful of the tiny wooden blocks.

Devon's eyes lit up. "That's perfect!" he affirmed. He addressed an imaginary audience. "Ladies and gentlemen, she's a genius!"

Elizabeth and Devon set to work assembling the instrument, making sure to follow Devon's diagram and formulas.

"And now the moment of truth," Devon said when they had finished. He hit one of the strings with the hammers they had created, and a rich, vibrating tone was produced.

"Hey, it works!" Elizabeth exclaimed, striking all the strings in succession. An off-key scale rang out. Narrowing his eyes, Devon adjusted a few of the dice. "Try it again," he encouraged her. Elizabeth quickly ran her hammer along the strings. This time the scale was almost perfect.

"Now all we've got to do is paint it, and we're done," Devon said, looking at the instrument in satisfaction. "But I think we should take a little break first."

"Hmmm," Elizabeth said, standing up and placing her hands on her hips. "What did you have in mind?"

"I'm sure we'll think of something," Devon said with a grin.

Wrapping her in his arms, he leaned in for a passionate kiss.

"There! It's finished!" Bruce exclaimed, the satisfaction plain in his voice.

Jessica looked up from her spot on the rug, where she was preparing a papier-mâché solution in a big bucket. Her eyes opened wide as she took in the monstrous wiry form on the floor. Bruce had constructed the frame of their volcano by twisting together long pieces of chicken wire. It was almost five feet tall and shaped like a fat pyramid.

"Um, that's great, Bruce," Jessica said, trying to sound encouraging. "I'm all ready too." Pouring a bit more oil into the bucket, Jessica stirred the mixture with a wooden spoon.

Bruce dropped a big stack of newspapers on the floor with a thud. Then he sat down across from Jessica. Picking up a paper, he began ripping off long, thin strips. "This is going to be great!" he enthused. "With a little bit of soapy water and dry ice, we can get it to foam and bubble just like a real volcano."

Jessica stirred the thick paste dubiously. She hoped Bruce was right. Jessica was beginning to wonder if they should take part in the fair at all. The only thing worse than letting Elizabeth and Devon win would be to let Devon see her looking like a fool.

Dipping her spoon into the bucket, Jessica drew out a spoonful of papier mâché and held it up. The mixture was thick and pasty, and it smelled slightly of glue. "OK, Bruce, I think this is done."

"You dip, I'll paste," Bruce suggested.

"Ready when you are," Jessica agreed.

Pulling on a pair of yellow rubber gloves, Jessica knelt down and reached for a strip of newspaper. She dipped it into the bucket, carefully wiping off the excess liquid. Bruce took the strip from her and pasted it onto the frame. Jessica handed him another piece, and he slapped it onto the volcano next to the first one.

Working as a team, they covered the entire frame in a matter of minutes.

Bruce smiled and patted the base lovingly. "Ah! She's going to be a real beauty!"

Jessica flinched at the sight of their project. Now it looked even more ghastly than it had before. "But it's bumpy," Jessica protested. "It looks like it has a disease."

Bruce scowled. "That's what volcanos are like," he insisted. "Don't you want this to look like the real thing?"

"Uh, yeah," Jessica agreed, wondering when Bruce had ever seen a five-foot volcano covered in pasty newspaper strips.

While the papier mâché was drying, Bruce led her to the basement to collect paint supplies. There was an entire toolshed in the cellar. A wooden workbench sat on the floor, and an assortment of hammers and wrenches hung from the walls. Jessica whistled softly. "Nice setup," she commented.

Bruce reached up on a shelf and lifted down a box. He opened the lid and peered inside. It was full of cans of paint and various-size brushes. "OK, let's go," he said.

When they got back upstairs, the frame was already dry. Bruce dropped the box on a table and stretched his arms above his head.

"How about if we paint it purple?" Jessica suggested. "We could even add tiny yellow flowers or moons."

Bruce shook his head. "Jessica, volcanoes are brown. And they don't have little moons on them."

"Brown?" Jessica asked in alarm. "You want to paint it *brown*?"

But Bruce was already wedging the lid off a can of brown paint. He pulled on a pair of gloves and stirred the paint carefully. Kneeling down in front of their creation, he dipped a paintbrush into the can and splashed it onto the side of the frame.

Sighing, Jessica picked up a paint can and knelt by his side. "If you can't beat 'em, join 'em," she muttered under her breath.

Twenty minutes later they were finished. The entire volcano was now painted a dark, molten brown. Jessica felt sick as she looked at it. She had a sinking feeling they were going to be the laughingstock of the school. *Devon will think I'm stupid,* she thought worriedly.

"Now for the coup de grâce!" Bruce exclaimed, inserting a funnel into the mouth of the volcano. He filled up a bucket with soap and water and added a few drops of red food coloring. Then he lifted the volcano and placed the bucket underneath the frame.

"OK," Bruce said, rubbing his hands together. "You ready for the moment of truth?"

Jessica nodded. "I guess so," she said.

Bruce pulled on a pair of thick thermal gloves and picked up a piece of dry ice. Tilting the volcano to one side, he carefully dropped the ice into the bucket. Then he replaced the frame and stepped back quickly.

The water began to hiss and spit. Jessica's eyes opened wide as steam started pouring out of the top in a thick red vapor. The pressure increased and foamy white bubbles spurted from the top.

"Hey! Wow!" Jessica exclaimed, clapping in delight. "How did you do that?"

"Simple," Bruce said with a shrug. "Dry ice is just frozen carbon dioxide. When you put it in water, it heats up quickly and is released as a gas."

"Bruce, I gotta hand it to you," Jessica said. "I'm impressed."

Bruce gave her a cocky smile. "I don't blame you."

Jessica stood back, taking in their creation in wonder. It really resembled a spouting volcano with hot, molten lava pouring out of the top. It looked like their project would be a success after all.

"Daddy's going to take me horseback riding next weekend in the country," Courtney said, her eyes shining with excitement.

"Hey, that's great," Todd responded in a lack-luster tone.

Todd and Courtney were out on a date on Friday night. She had invited him to her country club for dinner, and Todd had to sit through an excruciating formal meal with Courtney's parents. A bevy of black-tailed waiters fawned all over them, treating them like some kind of visiting royalty as they carried steaming, covered silver platters to their table.

Courtney's parents were nothing like his own. They were stiff and pretentious, with an affected manner of speaking that sounded vaguely British. They had spent the entire evening talking about an art auction in London. Todd had never been so bored in his life.

Now he and Courtney were sitting on lounge

chairs by the pool. The area was deserted except for two well-coiffed women playing mah-jongg at a table nearby. The women were wearing designer suits, and they looked like they'd had everything lifted, from their faces to their toes. Todd took a deep breath, feeling oppressed by the stuffy environment.

"Daddy has a whole stable of show horses," Courtney went on, crossing her long legs at the ankle. She flicked her hair back over her shoulder with a French-manicured fingernail. "Darling, his white stallion, took the gold medal at the horse races in Dover last year. They called him White Lightning in the British press." Courtney paused. "Daddy was just *thrilled*."

Todd gritted his teeth. If Courtney said "daddy" one more time, he was going to scream.

"When I was little, Daddy used to take me to the horse shows in Maine," Courtney continued. She reached for a glass of mineral water at her side.

Todd's eyes bulged. Clenching his jaw tight, he clawed at the side of his chair.

"Of course, now that I'm older, we only go to the best shows in Europe," Courtney said with a small, pretentious laugh. She pursed her red lips into a little *O* and took a sip out of her straw.

"Of course," Todd muttered, shifting impatiently in his seat.

Courtney smiled at him as she set her drink on the ground, his annoyance clearly lost on her.

"What a perfect evening!" Courtney murmured.

She stretched out lazily on the chair, revealing a pair of long tanned legs. Todd glanced over at her, finding himself strangely repulsed by her appearance. She wore a black silk halter dress, which bared her shoulders and highlighted her beautiful figure. But Todd found the outfit distasteful. All evening he'd felt like covering her up.

Courtney pulled herself to a sitting position, drawing her knees up to her chest. "The next time we go to Europe, we're going to go on a yacht cruise," she said.

Todd stifled a yawn. "Is that right?" he asked.

She nodded. "The best boats are anchored in the Mediterranean Sea. Of course, our yacht is in Monaco." Courtney clasped her hands around her knees, staring out at the pool with a dreamy expression on her face. "Daddy says the best time to go sailing is in the fall, when all the tourists are away."

Todd tuned out Courtney's chatter and leaned back in his chair. Her talk about the jet-set life was beginning to make him nauseous.

He stared up at the starless blue sky, realizing that this wasn't working for him. Courtney might be gorgeous, but she really wasn't his type. She was nice and friendly, but she was pretentious and superficial at the same time. Todd preferred Elizabeth's laid-back style. And her value system. And her heart.

Todd sighed, hit with a sudden insight. Despite everything that had happened, he was still in love with Elizabeth.

Chapter 11

"Welcome to Sweet Valley High's first annual science fair!" Mr. Russo announced in a booming voice on Saturday morning. He was standing on a platform in the field behind Sweet Valley High, a team of judges at his side.

A chorus of cheers greeted his announcement. Elizabeth smiled excitedly, swept up by the energy in the air. She was standing with Devon in the back of the crowd. It was a bright, beautiful day, and it looked like the science fair was going to a huge success. Almost everybody in the junior and senior classes had shown up.

"I'd like to introduce our panel of judges," Mr. Russo said, leaning into the microphone. "Please give a warm welcome to Mr. William Anderson, director of the American Science Association, and Mr. Theodore Baines, award-winning chemist and author of the book *Classic Science Projects*."

Mr. Anderson was a small, rotund man with bright blue eyes. He was wearing round red glasses and a flowered yellow tie. Mr. Baines, on the other hand, with his long, thin frame and scraggly beard, looked like a mad scientist.

The crowd roared its approval. Mr. Russo held up a hand to call for quiet. "I'd appreciate it if everybody would abide by the following conditions. First of all, each contestant must fill out an entry form. . . ."

Elizabeth tuned out Mr. Russo and glanced around the field, taking in the charged atmosphere. The science fair was turning out to be a real event. The lawn was dotted with colorful booths displaying the students' experiments. A long picnic table with chips and sodas stood at the edge of the grass. A couple of juniors had set up a barbecue grill, and the enticing aroma of smoky hot dogs and hamburgers wafted through the air.

The word *judges* reached her ears, and Elizabeth turned her attention back to Mr. Russo. "The judges will be coming around to examine each project individually," he was saying. "Your projects will be judged on scientific merit, innovativeness, form, and function. Each category is worth twenty-five points. You all should have received cards indicating your judging time. In the meantime you're free to mingle." Mr. Russo smiled at the crowd. "Enjoy the fair!"

"What a great turnout!" Elizabeth exclaimed as she and Devon headed back to their booth.

"I'll say," Devon agreed, running his fingers through his hair with a sigh.

Elizabeth glanced over at him worriedly. Devon was clearly uncomfortable. When they arrived, he had grabbed a booth way in the back and he'd been lying low all morning.

When they returned to their booth, they found that a crowd of interested onlookers had already gathered around. Their musical instrument was set out on a card table, the playing tools at its side. They had painted it a soft gold, giving it an antique look. Elizabeth had propped up a small sign in front of it. Using a quill pen, she had written the words *harmonious dulcimer* on it in Gothic lettering.

"Hey, is this some kind of ancient harp?" Annie Whitman asked, eyeing the instrument with curiosity. A sophomore with dark curly hair and green eyes, Annie was a member of the cheerleading squad and Pi Beta Alpha sorority.

"Something like that," Elizabeth said. "Except that you hit the strings instead of plucking them."

"Can we try it out?" Caroline Pearce asked.

"Sure!" Elizabeth said, handing Caroline one of the hammers. Caroline ran the playing tool along the strings. A rich chorus of notes came forth. "Wow, it's got a really beautiful sound," she breathed, hitting a few strings at random.

"This is sure to take first place," Olivia Davidson remarked. An artistic girl with an original sense of style, Olivia was the arts editor for the *Oracle* and a good friend of Elizabeth's.

Elizabeth looked at her with shining eyes. "Do you really think so?" she asked.

Olivia picked at a few strings with the hammer, listening as the delicate notes floated through the air. "Definitely," she affirmed.

"I was afraid of that," Devon said with a groan. He slumped down in his chair, pulling his baseball cap low over his forehead.

"This is way cool!" A. J. Morgan exclaimed, admiring Bruce and Jessica's project. He ran a hand through his curly red hair and leaned in for a closer inspection. The volcano was displayed prominently in a center booth. It had been running steadily for the past hour, hissing and sputtering, bubbly red steam gurgling forth from its mouth like hot lava.

"Thanks, man," Bruce said, smiling proudly.

A. J. knelt on the ground, bending his tall figure to listen to the rumbling coming from the volcano's belly. "How does it work?" he asked.

Bruce crouched by his side to explain.

Jessica's lips pulled down in a frown as the boys talked. Even though their volcano had turned out to be a success, Devon and Elizabeth's project was getting all the attention. A huge crowd was gathered around their table, and a rich melody could be heard as somebody composed a song.

Jessica scowled, drumming her fingers on the table. She'd thought she and Bruce had a chance, but now she was sure that Devon and Elizabeth would win the contest. After all, a real musical instrument was much more sophisticated than a fake volcano. *A volcano,* Jessica thought in disgust. *Why did I let Bruce talk me into this?*

Jessica kicked at a tuft of grass, her hands tightening into balls at her side. In the end Elizabeth would have everything—Devon Whitelaw, a moment of glory, and a romantic trip to San Francisco. And Jessica would have nothing. Nothing at all.

After A. J. left, Bruce stepped back and studied the volcano. The steam was fizzling out as the dry ice evaporated. A few loose wires poked out of the top.

"Should we add some more dry ice?" Jessica asked.

Bruce shook his head. "Not just yet," he said. "I think the pressure caused some of the wires to bust. I want to adjust them."

Bruce rummaged through their tool kit and pulled out a pair of red wire cutters. Climbing up on the table, he reached up to the top of the volcano and carefully twisted the loose wires back into place.

As Jessica watched Bruce work she was suddenly struck with a brilliant thought.

161

"There we go!" Bruce said, jumping down from the table.

Jessica turned to him, an evil smile on her face. "Bruce, can I borrow those for a minute?"

"Sure, Jess," Bruce said distractedly, handing her the wire cutters.

"Thanks," she said sweetly, turning to go. "I'll be right back."

"I can't believe I'm actually at a *science fair*," Courtney complained, flipping her thick hair back over her shoulders. "What a total bore."

You're a total bore, Todd thought, sick of Courtney's whining. She had been complaining nonstop ever since they arrived.

But Todd refused to let his impatience show. Even if he had realized that Courtney wasn't the one for him, he wanted everybody to think that they were the perfect couple. After all, everyone now knew that Elizabeth and Devon were together. They were walking around hand in hand, gazing at each other like lovesick puppies. Todd didn't want to look pathetic in front of the entire school.

Despite the fact that Elizabeth was throwing her new relationship in his face, Todd had only one thought in mind. He was more determined than ever to get her back.

Wrapping an arm around Courtney's waist, he drew her closer to him. "C'mon, it's not so bad," he said. "After all, we're here together."

Courtney lifted her hand to her mouth in an exaggerated yawn. "I guess so," she said with a sigh.

Pulling out a little gold compact and a tube of crimson lipstick from her purse, Courtney pursed her lips and retouched them. She smacked her lips together and threw the compact back in her bag. "Well, I guess we might as well go check out Lila and Amy's project," she said. "After all, that's why we're here."

A number of students were huddled around Lila and Amy's booth, and shouts of laughter were coming from the group. Todd and Courtney wove their way through the crowd to the front.

Lila and Amy had made a miniature silver robot that was powered by a handheld remote control. She was bald, with light blue eye shadow on her wide eyelids and full red lips. She was dressed at the moment in a gold lamé dress. A comic sign was set up on the table. It featured a picture of the model with an exaggerated look of distress on her face. A thought bubble hovered above her head with the words *I'm a slave to fashion!* written on it.

Todd watched as Lila directed the little automated figure with the remote. The model turned slowly, revealing the dress at different angles. Then she walked down the miniature runway, swishing her hips forward. The onlookers clapped in pleasure.

After the show was over, most of the students wandered away. "So what do you think?" Lila asked breathlessly, turning her attention to Todd and Courtney.

"I'm very impressed," Todd enthused. "Your little android is really great—it walks just like a real person."

Amy giggled, her gray eyes bright with excitement. "Todd, how did you guess? Her name is Androida."

"Is Androida androgynous?" Courtney asked, picking up the sleek silver figure and examining it.

Amy shook her head. "No, of course not. She's a female fashion model."

Courtney frowned. "But why doesn't she have any hair?"

Lila grinned. "It's a very chic look. The latest thing in fashion."

Todd tuned the girls out, searching the crowd for Elizabeth. He caught sight of her with Devon at a corner booth. They were standing in front of their project, their backs toward Todd. Devon's hand rested lightly on Elizabeth's waist, and she stood close to him.

Todd felt himself heating up with anger. It made him crazy to see Elizabeth with that jerk. He wanted to march over to them and pummel the guy for touching Elizabeth that way.

But Todd forced himself to stay calm. If he wanted to get Elizabeth back, he couldn't lose his cool.

He clenched his jaw and turned to Courtney.

Holding out his arm chivalrously, he gave her a dashing smile. "So, should we continue to make the rounds?"

"Do you want to take a look around?" Elizabeth asked Devon, glancing down at their card. She and Devon had the last spot of the afternoon. They wouldn't be judged until three o'clock.

Devon hopped up quickly, suddenly infused with new energy. "Yeah, that's a great idea," he agreed.

Elizabeth bit her lip, wondering if enrolling in the fair had been such a good idea after all. Devon was obviously stressed about all the attention they were receiving.

As if he could read her thoughts, Devon took her hand and kissed her softly on the cheek. "Don't worry about me," he reassured her. "I'm fine."

Elizabeth whistled softly as she and Devon made their way through the crowded field. They were both impressed with the displays. The students had come up with really creative, sophisticated projects. Sandra Bacon and Jean West had created a rainbow on a screen through the use of a large prism catching the rays of the sun, and Ken Matthews and Bill Chase had made a magic mirror that distorted any images reflected in it.

As she and Devon wandered from one booth to the next, Elizabeth found herself thinking about Todd. She was painfully aware of his presence at the fair, and she was having a hard time enjoying herself because of it. Todd, on the other hand, seemed perfectly at ease with the new situation. He was obviously very happy with Courtney Kane.

Elizabeth caught sight of the two of them across the field, and she couldn't help feeling a twinge of jealousy. They were holding hot dogs and laughing together. Courtney was waving an animated hand in the air, flipping back her thick mane of hair. Even though Elizabeth found Courtney to be boring and superficial, she couldn't help noticing how classically beautiful she was.

Courtney whispered something in Todd's ear, and he laughed softly. Then he leaned over and kissed her on the cheek.

Elizabeth felt a sharp pang. Wrenching her eyes away, she turned her attention back to Devon.

"Hey, Liz! Over here!" a female voice yelled. Shading her eyes from the sun, Elizabeth looked in the direction of the voice. Maria Slater was waving in her direction.

Grateful for the distraction, Elizabeth waved back. She grabbed Devon's hand and pulled him over toward Maria's booth.

Elizabeth's eyes widened at the sight of Maria and Enid's project. The girls had made a revolving carousel out of plastic straws. Instead of seats, huge soap bubbles hung from the ends of the rectangular cross sections of the wheel. The entire spectrum of the rainbow seemed to be reflected in the bubbles.

"Wow, this is beautiful!" Elizabeth exclaimed. "But what is it?"

"It's a soap bubble Ferris wheel," Enid said proudly, her green eyes sparkling. She turned the wire crank connected to the side, causing the bubbles to revolve. They shimmered iridescently in the afternoon sunlight.

Devon cocked his head. "Pretty impressive," he put in. "This is a great test of the use of molecular force."

Maria winked. "Tell that to the judges," she said with a grin.

"What about us?" Winston called out from the next booth. As usual Winston had gotten into the spirit of things. He was dressed like a barker in red plaid pants and a little felt cap. Winston picked up a big megaphone and held it up to his mouth. "Step right up, everybody! Step right up!"

Elizabeth laughed as she and Devon headed for the booth, amused at the ridiculous figure that Winston cut.

Maria Santelli shook her head as she watched Winston. "I just don't know what to do with him," she said with a mock sigh.

"Well, at least you're getting good publicity," Devon put in with a grin.

Elizabeth gazed at Winston and Maria's sophisticated project. "Devon, look at this," she murmured in appreciation.

Winston and Maria had made a miniature

waterwheel. Water from an angled spout spilled onto a revolving wheel, which then emptied into a gutter underneath. "Wow, I am impressed," Elizabeth said. She leaned in closer to examine the project. "But how does it work?"

"These are snail shells," Winston explained, pointing to the tiny shells attached to the wheel. "When the jet of water from the spout hits the openings of the shells, they fill up and move downward under the pressure, causing the wheel to turn."

"This is great, you guys," Devon said happily. "I think you've got this competition in the bag."

"Bruce, the judges are on their way!" Jessica exclaimed, watching as Mr. Anderson and Mr. Baines headed across the lawn toward them. "Is everything ready?" she asked, pacing across the grass nervously.

"Chill out, Wakefield," Bruce said, standing back with a cocky expression on his face. "She looks great."

The volcano was in fine form, rocking and spurting as a fresh stream of bubbly vapor poured out of its mouth. A foamy mist floated around the top, giving the impression of a volcano lost in the clouds.

Jessica bit her lip. "I guess you're right," she agreed.

But as the judges approached their stand, the

hissing got lower and the bubbly stream pouring out of the top got thinner. The vapor in the air began to evaporate. With a final hiss the volcano rocked to a complete stop.

Jessica's eyes popped wide open. "Bruce, quick, we need some more dry ice!"

Bruce looked at her in alarm. "But we don't have any more here. The rest is in my car."

"What? You didn't bring any more?" Jessica asked in an accusing tone.

"Me?" Bruce exclaimed. "*I'm* the one who carried the volcano across the field. *You* were the one who was supposed to worry about supplies."

Jessica stamped her foot in frustration. "Look, there's no use throwing around blame now. We've got to get more dry ice. And fast."

"Fine!" Bruce returned, sending her a withering look. "I'll be right back." He turned around and took off across the field.

Just then the judges appeared. "Very nice," Mr. Anderson commented, scratching his chin carefully as he studied their creation. "You've constructed a volcanic form out of chicken wire and papier mâché."

Mr. Baines smiled, his blue eyes friendly. "And you've made it almost life-size as well."

Mr. Anderson pulled out a form, scanned it quickly, and took a seat in one of the chairs at the booth. "Now, Miss . . . Wakefield," he said, reading her name off the entry form. "Would you like to explain the basic principles governing the functioning of your experiment?" He sat back and crossed his legs, looking at her expectantly.

Jessica swallowed hard. "Well, the basic principle is one of, um, evaporation." She racked her brains, trying to remember what Bruce had told her. "Dry ice is simply, uh—" She hesitated, feeling herself break out in a cold sweat. Then the words came to her. "Frozen carbon monoxide," she supplied quickly.

"Carbon *dioxide*," Mr. Baines corrected her gently, sitting down in a chair next to Mr. Anderson.

"Right, carbon dioxide," Jessica said, giving the judges a charming smile. "So when we place a block of dry ice in water, the carbon dioxide transforms from a frozen to a gaseous state. It melts immediately, releasing a vapor into the air." Jessica let her breath out in a rush.

"Very well put," Mr. Anderson said, smiling at her approvingly. He scribbled a few notes on his form.

Jessica smiled back, glancing nervously across the yard. If Bruce didn't show up soon, they weren't going to have any experiment to perform at all. She breathed a sigh of relief as she caught sight of him flying across the lawn, a bucket of dry ice in his hand.

Bruce arrived at the booth out of breath. "Hello!" he greeted the judges. He set the bucket down on the ground, panting.

"You must be Mr. Patman," Mr. Baines said.

Bruce nodded. "Nice to meet you," he said, holding out a hand.

Mr. Anderson looked up from his form. "Your partner has just given us a very impressive explanation of the chemical functioning of your project."

Bruce lifted an eyebrow, and Jessica shot him an angry look.

"So are you ready to perform a demonstration?" Mr. Baines asked.

Jessica nodded, grabbing the bucket and kneeling on the ground. Bruce crouched down next to her, lifting the base of the volcano. Pulling on a pair of thermal gloves, Jessica reached for a block of dry ice and dropped it carefully into the bucket. The soapy water began to sizzle immediately. Jessica reached for another block of dry ice.

"One is enough," Bruce hissed at her.

"Shhh!" Jessica responded. "We've got to go all out this time." She quickly plopped two more blocks in the water. The water began to fizzle, and Bruce dropped the base over the bucket.

Jessica watched nervously as the volcano roared to life. A sharp hissing sound began from the inside. Suddenly huge red bubbles began pouring through the opening on the top. Jessica smiled in satisfaction.

The display was magnificent. The steam shot through the top with great force, capturing the effect of a real, high-pressure volcano spouting red-hot lava. A crowd gathered around quickly, oohing and ahhing at the impressive demonstration.

Jessica turned to Bruce, a triumphant expression on her face. "See?" she exclaimed.

But as soon as she had gotten the word out, an ominous rumbling sound came from the base. Red steam shot through the top at full speed, and large pieces of papier mâché began to fly off the sides. Spurts of steam sizzled out of the top and the sides as well. Suddenly the entire bucket of water burst through the holes in the frame, sending a powerful spray of soapy water across the lawn.

Everybody stared in astonishment.

Mr. Anderson crinkled his brow in consternation. "Hmmm," he said, scratching his chin. "Well, we can give you a twenty-five for creativity."

"Oh, no!" Elizabeth exclaimed, clapping her hand over her mouth as soapy water sprayed forth from Jessica and Bruce's volcano. It was like a huge water balloon bursting open at the seams.

"Well, they've certainly pulled off an explosive experiment," Devon remarked ironically.

Soapy red water ran in thick rivulets across the grass. Students were slipping and sliding, and peals of laughter shook the air. A small water fight had broken out near the volcano. Jessica and Bruce were standing by the booth, their mouths dropped open in shock.

"Do you want to go check it out?" Devon asked.

"Actually we'd better get back to our booth," Elizabeth said, glancing at her watch. "The judges are coming to us next."

Devon sighed, shifting his weight from one foot to the other. "OK, let's go," he said.

"Hey, you're not getting cold feet, are you?" Elizabeth asked, turning to face him.

Devon nodded, looking abashed. "Actually I am. You know how I feel about unwanted attention." Then he cheered up. "C'mon, it's time to face the music."

"Or play the music," Elizabeth said with a smile.

They hurried back to their booth, careful to avoid the wet spots in the lawn. Elizabeth took her place behind their instrument and picked up one of the hammers. "Do you think we should play when they show up?"

Devon nodded. "Yeah, we should probably run through a few scales." He rubbed his chin thoughtfully. "I wonder if Maria could play one of her songs as well."

Gazing across the field to see if the judges were on their way, Elizabeth ran her hammer along the strings. The notes rang out in a strange succession. Blinking, Elizabeth looked down at the dulcimer. Two of the strings were dangling loose. Elizabeth examined them in alarm. They appeared to have been torn in the middle.

"Devon!" Elizabeth gasped. "Two of the strings are broken!"

"What?" Devon exclaimed, hurrying to her side. Frowning, he fingered the strings.

"Do we have any more wire?" Elizabeth asked.

Devon shook his head ruefully.

Elizabeth searched frantically for a solution. "Can we can repair the strings?" she asked quickly, looking at him hopefully.

But Devon shook his head. "Even if we managed to fuse the wires, the cracks would ruin the sound." Devon picked up one of the wires in his hand and studied it. "You know, Elizabeth, this wire didn't break," he said, his eyes narrowed. "It's been cut."

Elizabeth's eyes popped open in shock. "Somebody sabotaged our project?" she exclaimed.

Devon nodded, his expression grim. "It looks like it."

Elizabeth's heart sank. After all their work, their project was worthless. She couldn't believe that anybody would stoop so low as to pull a stunt like this. She glanced at Devon worriedly, sure that he would be steaming mad.

But to Elizabeth's surprise, he began to laugh.

"Devon?" she asked, her eyes widening.

But Devon just tilted back his head and laughed and laughed.

Chapter 12

"What a total disaster," Jessica muttered to herself on Sunday morning after breakfast. She and Elizabeth were sitting outside on the patio by the Wakefields' in-ground swimming pool. In order to make up for her neglect during the week, Mrs. Wakefield had prepared a big Sunday brunch of blueberry pancakes and homemade muffins.

Now the girls were alone, catching the first rays of the early afternoon sun. The sun was shining, but the air felt heavy with the promise of rain. A few ominous-looking clouds were moving slowly across the sky.

"What's a total disaster?" Elizabeth asked in a mellow voice. She lay stretched out on a chaise lounge in a yellow racing suit, her face turned lazily to the sun.

"*Everything*," Jessica grumbled, swinging her

legs around the side of the chair and standing up. She adjusted the straps of her new tangerine-colored bikini and started to pace the white pavement.

Jessica was seething in frustration. All her plans had been thwarted. The science fair was a total bust. After all the work that she and Bruce had put into their project, the volcano had completely exploded. *Well, we certainly got a lot of attention,* Jessica thought. But instead of thinking she was brilliant, now Devon probably thought she was a total idiot. Jessica frowned. Her attempts to ruin Elizabeth and Devon's project had been equally unsuccessful. Instead of being upset about the snipped wires, Devon was thrilled. Now he and Elizabeth were just as happy as ever.

There had been a big awards ceremony at the end of the day. Winston and Maria's waterwheel had taken first prize, and Lila and Amy's robot had come in second. A couple of sophomores who made a model solar home had been awarded third prize. Jessica and Bruce had received a red ribbon for creativity.

Jessica scowled, clenching her hands at her sides. Not only had her plan for revenge failed, but it had completely backfired. Instead of causing Elizabeth and Devon to break up, Jessica had only succeeded in creating two perfect couples. "It's like Noah's ark around here," she muttered under her breath.

"What did you say?" Elizabeth asked, opening her eyes and looking in Jessica's direction.

"Nothing," Jessica responded sullenly. She took a seat on the edge of her chair.

Elizabeth sat up and reached for her sunglasses. "Are you still upset about the science fair?" she asked. Pushing on her sunglasses, she picked up a glass of lemonade from the small table at her side.

Jessica shrugged, leaning over to adjust the chaise lounge to a reclining position. The air was thick with humidity, and she could feel beads of perspiration gathering along her forehead. Sitting back in her chair, she mopped off her hot face with her towel.

"Don't feel so bad about it, Jessica," Elizabeth said in a reassuring tone. "Your volcano was a huge success—until it, um, exploded." Fanning her face lightly, Elizabeth held her glass against her cheek.

"It's not that," Jessica countered. "It's just that I'm sick of being surrounded by all these *couples* all of a sudden." She squeezed a handful of suntan lotion onto her palm.

Elizabeth frowned. "You mean Todd and Courtney—?" she asked.

Jessica nodded. "It's just all sooo cozy," she complained. "Next thing you know, you're going to be giving back that ring so that Todd can give it to Courtney." Leaning over, she began spreading lotion on her legs.

177

Elizabeth started to laugh, but then she stopped. "Hey, it's a crazy idea, but it's not a bad one." She set her glass down on the ground, a thoughtful look on her face.

"What?" Jessica asked, startled. "Yes, it is," she said quickly. "It's a very bad idea." She sat up straight, lifting her heavy hair off the nape of her neck and twisting it into a bun.

"Well, I don't really like the thought of seeing my special gift on Courtney's hand," Elizabeth conceded, "but it's certainly one way of showing my approval of Todd and Courtney. Todd would realize that there aren't any hard feelings between us."

"But it's not Courtney's style at all!" Jessica protested quickly. "She's not a writer. She'd never wear it."

Elizabeth shrugged. "I don't think you have to be a writer to wear that ring. It's a classic design. Any girl would love it."

Jessica gaped at her sister. "Elizabeth, I wasn't serious," she protested. A few loose strands of hair fell across her neck, and she tucked them back into her bun.

"Well, I am," Elizabeth responded. She reached for the cordless phone on the table.

Jessica's eyes widened as Elizabeth punched in Todd's number.

"Hi, Todd, it's Liz," Elizabeth said, holding the receiver up to her ear. She stood up and took a few steps across the white pavement. The sky darkened, and the first few raindrops pattered to the ground.

Elizabeth crossed one leg in front of the other, glancing up at the sky in alarm. "Um, I was wondering if you were free for lunch. There's something I want to discuss with you."

She listened for a moment, and then she nodded. "The Dairi Burger? In half an hour? See you there."

Jessica's mouth fell open in horror. If Todd and Elizabeth started talking about the ring, they were bound to figure out that it hadn't been Elizabeth who was wearing it that day in the school parking lot. And what about the day when Todd had taken Courtney to Guido's and then Jessica had conveniently called Elizabeth and asked her to meet her there . . . and then Jessica hadn't even been there when Elizabeth had arrived? Todd and Elizabeth were gullible, but they weren't stupid. They'd figure out what had really happened in about five seconds, and then they'd be out for blood.

Elizabeth clicked off the phone and set it down on the table. Grabbing her bathing suit cover-up, she headed for the back door.

Jessica scrambled out of her chair. "Wait! Elizabeth! You can't do this!" she objected. A few raindrops hit her squarely on her cheeks, and she brushed them away.

Elizabeth turned back at the door, a look of impatience on her face. "If I didn't know better, I would think you wanted me and Todd to be enemies."

"No, of course not," Jessica said, thinking

quickly. "I just don't think this is a good idea. You're going to end up hurting Todd's feelings."

Elizabeth shook her head firmly. "No, I won't. He's got somebody else now."

"But—but—," Jessica sputtered. A streak of yellow heat lightning flashed across the dark sky, illuminating it suddenly.

"See you later," Elizabeth said, cutting her off. She swung open the screen door and disappeared behind it.

Jessica gaped at the door, mentally kicking herself. *Why did you have to open your big mouth?* she berated herself. This whole situation was unbearable.

A bolt of thunder rocked the sky, followed by a gust of wind. The clouds suddenly let forth with a burst of rain. Jessica quickly grabbed her towel and hurried across the patio, fat raindrops hitting her in the face.

Jessica pulled open the door frantically. She had to do something. Immediately.

"So what did you want to talk about, Liz?" Todd asked.

Elizabeth glanced up at him, hesitating. She and Todd sat in a wooden booth at the front of the Dairi Burger, drinking cappuccinos. The storm had been short and sudden. Now a light rain fell against the windowpane, enveloping them in a private, padded universe.

Elizabeth swallowed hard as she looked into Todd's familiar brown eyes. Suddenly she was hit with a sense of nostalgia. She and Todd had often come to the Dairi Burger on Sunday mornings. It had been one of their favorite places for brunch. On the surface it seemed as if nothing had changed. And yet now they were almost strangers to each other.

"Elizabeth?" Todd prodded.

Elizabeth took a deep breath. "I . . . I just wanted to let you know that I'm really happy for you, Todd," she said, the words coming out in a rush. "For you and Courtney."

Elizabeth felt a strange pain shoot through her chest, and she realized that she was lying. She wasn't happy for Todd and Courtney. She was sick about it. She couldn't get over the feeling that Todd was hers.

"Uh, thanks," Todd responded, coughing uncomfortably. "I appreciate it." He picked up his cup of cappuccino and stared out at the misty sky, an unreadable expression on his face.

Elizabeth wondered suddenly if she was making a big mistake. Was she losing her mind? Did she really want to push Todd into the arms of another girl?

But the wheels were already in motion. She had started this, and she had to go through with it. Without allowing herself to think about it any further, Elizabeth reached into her bag and pulled out

181

the blue velvet box that Todd had given her. Reluctantly she opened it up and took out the ring. The delicate silver band gleamed brightly in her hand.

"I wanted to give this back to you," Elizabeth said, holding it out to Todd. "It's so beautiful, I'm sure Courtney would love it." An unexpected tear came to her eye, and she blinked it back quickly.

Todd drew back as if he had been hit, a look of total bewilderment on his face. Then he frowned and shook his head. "No, I don't want it back," he said firmly. "I gave it to you, and I want you to have it."

"Todd, I can't wear it," Elizabeth insisted. "It's just not right." She pressed the ring into his hand.

"But you *did* wear it," Todd countered, folding the ring in his hand and tucking it in his pocket. A rumble of thunder sounded off in the distance, and a heavy rain began to fall. A gust of wind shot through the front door. Todd twisted around and reached for the jacket hanging over the back of his chair.

"No, I didn't," Elizabeth responded. "What are you talking about?" Shivering slightly, she pulled her sweater tighter around her.

"That day after school, when I was sitting with Courtney and you waved to me, you were wearing the ring," Todd explained, shrugging on his jacket.

Elizabeth frowned. "What day after school?"

Todd gave her an odd look. "Wednesday afternoon," he said, cupping his hands around his mug of cappuccino. "You were coming from the *Oracle* office. I was sitting with Courtney on the steps outside."

Elizabeth shook her head in confusion. "I never saw you and Courtney. I was totally shock—I mean *surprised* to see you together at Guido's."

Todd's eyes opened wide. "You saw us at Guido's?" he asked. A shadow of guilt crossed his face.

Elizabeth nodded uncomfortably. She looked down quickly, fiddling with her long teaspoon. How had things gotten so complicated all of a sudden?

"I—we—," Todd sputtered, his face turning bright red.

Elizabeth held up a hand. "It's OK. You don't have to explain." But somewhere deep inside, she couldn't help hoping that he would. She still didn't understand how he could have rebounded so fast. And she couldn't help wishing that he still loved her after all.

But Todd was frowning and looking out into space. "I'm *sure* it was you," he insisted. "I thought you were sending me a message. I just can't understand it."

Elizabeth frowned as well. "It doesn't make any sense," she agreed. "You always recognize me. You never confuse me with . . ."

Elizabeth stared straight at Todd, suddenly catching on.

"Jessica!" they exclaimed in unison.

✧   ✧   ✧

"Courtney, step on the gas!" Jessica urged, her chest tight with anxiety.

"OK, OK!" Courtney responded, pushing down hard on the accelerator.

Jessica and Courtney were barreling toward the Dairi Burger in Courtney's white Mustang convertible. They were on Valley Crest Road, and the wet trees were whizzing by in a blur. The windows were rolled down slightly, causing a whistling wind to rush through the car.

Frantic, Jessica had called Courtney as soon as Elizabeth had left. "I need you to pick me up immediately!" she had cried. "It's urgent."

Ten minutes later Courtney had pulled up to the sidewalk outside the Wakefield house. She had clearly just run out of the house. Even though she was usually dressed impeccably, today she was wearing a simple black T-shirt dress and flat black pumps. Her thick chestnut hair was in disarray, falling in tangled waves around her shoulders. The only makeup she had on was a light coat of mauve lipstick.

Jessica was dressed casually as well. She had pulled on her favorite pair of faded jeans, white tennis shoes with no socks, and a blue shirt with a rounded neck. At the last minute she had thrown her cheerleading jacket over her shoulders. Her hair was pulled back in a loose ponytail.

They reached a bend in the road, and Courtney put her foot on the brakes, screeching around the turn. The road glistened dangerously in front of them. With an effort Courtney straightened out the wheels and continued down the street. "So what is this all about?" she asked.

A few raindrops flew into the car, and Jessica rolled up her window. "There's something going on at the Dairi Burger that I think you need to know about," she explained. She shifted in her seat, tapping a foot impatiently on the floor.

"But what?" Courtney pressed, squinting to see through the rain. She flicked on her windshield wipers and slowed down slightly. Braking carefully, she turned onto the road leading to the Dairi Burger.

Jessica's expression was grim. "It's Todd and Elizabeth," she said solemnly. "I think they're getting back together."

"What?" Courtney exclaimed in shock. Ignoring the slippery road, she pushed her foot all the way to the floor. The car took off with a jolt and flew down the street. A passing motorist honked his car horn in disapproval.

Courtney slammed on the brakes as they reached the Dairi Burger. The car swerved dangerously, and the girls flew forward. Jessica felt her seat belt tighten around her waist. "Courtney, watch out!" Jessica exclaimed. "Do you want to get us killed?"

"I got us here, didn't I?" Courtney asked, fire in her eyes.

Turning the wheels sharply to the left, Courtney squealed into the parking lot, drove across the gravel, and screeched into a spot. Jessica heaved a sigh of relief as they came to a bumpy stop. She had wanted Courtney to drive quickly, but she hadn't expected her to turn into a total maniac. Taking a long breath to calm her nerves, Jessica pulled her jacket tightly around her and jumped out of the car.

Courtney was waiting for her outside, her expression grim. "OK, let's go," she said. She squared her shoulders and headed determinedly across the lot.

Jessica hurried after her. Just as they reached the restaurant she heard the familiar sound of a motorcycle rushing into the lot. Jessica turned to see Devon pulling into a spot by the door, a harsh look on his face.

Good, Jessica thought. *Everything is going according to plan.*

"Jessica kept telling me to go for revenge," Todd admitted, stabbing at a piece of cantaloupe with his fork and bringing it to his mouth.

The storm had picked up again, and Elizabeth and Todd had moved to a corner booth in the back of the restaurant. Todd had ordered a bowl of fresh fruit and another cup of coffee. Still full from breakfast, Elizabeth had just asked for a glass of herbal tea.

Rain fell in steady streams against the windows, blanketing the sounds of the crowd. Despite the bad weather the restaurant was packed with young people. Students were talking and laughing in the cozy wooden booths, and pings and beeps sounded from the game room. Known for its big omelets and home fries, the Dairi Burger was one of the most popular spots for Sunday brunch among Sweet Valley students.

"I can't believe it," Elizabeth breathed. Suddenly everything was becoming clear to her. Jessica had never forgiven her in the first place. She had been trying to sabotage Elizabeth and Devon's relationship all week.

Jessica must have orchestrated the whole thing with Courtney, she realized. She must have set her up to catch Courtney and Todd at Guido's. Elizabeth shook her head in disgust. How could she have been so naive?

"She wanted me to make you jealous so things wouldn't work out with you and Devon," Todd continued. He pushed around the fruit in his bowl with his fork.

Elizabeth looked down, feeling her face flush. "Actually I was," she admitted. She picked up her napkin and twisted it in her lap. Then she looked up and caught Todd's eye. "And I still am," she added.

"Then you still . . . care?" Todd asked softly.

Elizabeth nodded, feeling her eyes moisten.

Todd leaned across the table and took her hand in his. Elizabeth felt a well of confusion mount in her. It was so warm and familiar with Todd, as if nothing had changed between them. And yet she knew in her heart that she still wanted to be with Devon.

Suddenly Elizabeth heard the sound of footsteps approaching. She turned around and gasped. Jessica and Courtney stood a few feet from their table. And Devon was one step behind them, a look of pure venom on his face.

"Elizabeth," Devon began, pushing past Jessica and Courtney. But his words dropped off suddenly as he glanced down at the table, where Elizabeth's hand was intertwined with Todd's. Devon took a step back, the color draining from his face.

Elizabeth yanked her hand away from Todd's. "It's not what it looks like," she whispered desperately.

Chapter 13

"Get your hands off her!" Devon ordered Todd, his voice filled with rage. He was standing with his feet wide apart, his fists clenched at his sides.

Todd scraped back his chair and stood up to meet him. "Don't you *dare* tell me what to do," he responded, his eyes narrowed in fury.

An angry nerve twitched in Devon's jaw. "Why don't you let her go?" he asked in a low voice. "Don't you know that she's ready for someone new?"

"We were doing just fine together until a second ago," Todd retorted.

Momentary pain flickered across Devon's face. He glanced at Elizabeth for confirmation, but she just sat in her seat, gaping at the boys in shock. This was a confrontation out of her worst nightmares.

A breeze shook through an open window, and Todd flipped his head back, whipping his hair off his forehead. "You couldn't possibly understand what Elizabeth and I mean to each other," he exclaimed. His cheeks flushed a deep red.

Devon rolled his eyes. "Not anymore, Wilkins. It's over. Can't you understand that?"

"It's not over," Todd replied in a strangled whisper. "Elizabeth and I are going to be together forever." He turned and faced her with imploring eyes. "Aren't we, Liz?"

Elizabeth felt her heart wrench at Todd's desperate plea. She opened her mouth to respond, but she found herself at a loss for words. She couldn't say yes, but she couldn't say no either. Not in front of everybody.

Devon grabbed Todd by the arm. "Would you stop it?" he said, his voice dripping with disdain. "You're pathetic."

Devon's gesture seemed to catapult Todd into action. "Get out of my way," he growled.

Todd turned to Elizabeth and fell down on one knee in front of her. He reached into his pocket and pulled out the ring. His deep brown eyes overflowing with tenderness, he held the sparkling silver band out to her. "Elizabeth, will you marry me?" he whispered.

Elizabeth gasped, feeling the blood drain from her face. Was Todd losing his mind? The others looked on in shocked silence. "Todd," Elizabeth whispered, but she didn't know what to say. She felt dangerously on the edge of tears.

Devon broke the silence. He grabbed Todd by the arm and yanked him violently up to his feet. "I've had enough of this!" he yelled.

Todd pushed him back. "*I'm* the one who's had enough," he shouted. "If you knew what was good for you, you'd go away—far away. You'd leave town just the way you came."

Devon crossed his arms over his chest. "Is that a threat?" he asked quietly.

"Yes," Todd answered, taking a few menacing steps forward. "It is."

Devon shoved him on the chest. "I've told you before, Wilkins, nobody threatens me," he said.

Todd shoved him back. "Well, there's always a first time," he retorted.

Devon pushed Todd hard, and he slammed into the table, knocking a pitcher of water to the ground. There was a sound of shattering glass and Todd whirled around, his fists clenched. Todd gave Devon a sharp hook to the jaw, and Devon responded by punching him in the gut. Todd recoiled, wrapping his arms around his stomach. Gritting his teeth, he flew full force at Devon.

"Stop it!" Elizabeth screamed, jumping up in horror. "Stop it!" What was going on? Todd was usually so gentle, and Devon was so refined. Now the two of them were rolling around on the floor like a pair of wild beasts.

A crowd of students had gathered around to watch. "Fight! Fight! Fight!" they chanted.

Elizabeth grabbed her head with her hands, feeling as if she were caught in some horrible nightmare. "Somebody stop them!" she cried.

But the crowd just continued its low chanting. The rhythmic words echoed the loud beating of Elizabeth's heart.

Panicked, Elizabeth dropped to the ground and tried to pull the boys apart herself. But they seemed to be completely unaware of her. A fist brushed her jaw, and Elizabeth recoiled in fear. Then a foot knocked her in the side. A searing pain traveled across her rib cage. Gasping, Elizabeth tried to catch her breath.

Suddenly she felt two strong arms pulling her back. It was Tim Nelson, the defensive linebacker of the Gladiators, the Sweet Valley High football team.

"Break it up!" a couple of football players were shouting. Tad Johnson and Robbie Hendricks jumped in and forcibly pulled the boys apart.

"Are you all right?" Tim asked Elizabeth, dropping his hold on her.

Elizabeth nodded, her whole body trembling. Stepping to the side, she wrapped her arms around herself.

She felt a pair of angry eyes boring into her and turned to see Courtney glaring at her. "I hope you're happy," Courtney said icily.

Elizabeth backed away. She had already been beaten up physically. Her cheek was sore, and her ribs ached. She didn't need mental abuse as well.

Elizabeth glanced up, hot tears beginning to flow down her cheeks. Todd and Devon were being restrained by the guys from the team, but they both looked like they would lunge forward and kill each other if they could break free. Devon struggled furiously, waving his arms around wildly.

"Let me go!" Todd groaned, angry sparks shooting from his eyes.

Shaking with fury, Elizabeth turned to face them. "Stop it! Both of you!" The crowd quieted down as Elizabeth spoke. "You're both animals!" she lashed out. "I don't want to have anything to do with either of you!"

Elizabeth pivoted on her heel and stormed away.

Late that afternoon Courtney paced the floor of her pale pink room. *Stupid, stupid, stupid,* she repeated to herself. She tangled her hands in her hair as if she wanted to rip it out of her head.

Why don't you ever learn? she berated herself, burning a path on the plush beige carpet. *Why are you so gullible?* Once again Todd had used her to make Elizabeth jealous. And once again Todd had chosen Elizabeth over her.

Courtney sank down into an antique chair, feeling completely and utterly betrayed. She thought of her date with Todd at the pizza parlor. She remembered how he had sat close by her side and how he had enticed her with his flattery and attention. And she remembered his passionate kisses.

"It was all a lie," Courtney whispered to herself. She curled her hands into tiny angry fists. *All a lie.*

Now she had been burned not once but twice by Todd Wilkins—and by Elizabeth too. Courtney stood up and went to the window. Pulling open the curtains, she stared out at the darkening sky. Now she really was out for revenge. Somehow. Sometime.

"I'm sorry, Elizabeth can't come to the phone right now," Jessica said wearily into the receiver later that afternoon. It was Todd, and this was the third time he had called.

The phone had been ringing over and over at the Wakefields' all day. Todd for Elizabeth. Devon for Elizabeth. Maria for Elizabeth.

But Elizabeth had shut herself up in her room and wouldn't talk to anyone. When Jessica had gotten home, she had pounded on her sister's door. But Elizabeth had locked herself in. "Go away!" she had ordered. "I never want to speak to you again."

Now Jessica could hear her sister crying bitterly. Elizabeth had been sobbing all afternoon. At times resounding thuds came from the room, as if Elizabeth were throwing things at the wall. Each new outburst caused Jessica to wince.

"Are you sure you're telling me the truth?" Todd bit out. His voice was bitter and accusing.

Jessica heaved a deep sigh. "Todd, I'm sorry, she won't talk to anyone." She waded through a pile of clothes on the floor, dragging the phone cord behind her.

"Fine, I'll try again later," Todd responded in a clipped voice. Then he slammed down the phone.

Jessica flinched at Todd's angry gesture. Kicking a shirt out of her way, she cleared a path to the nightstand and replaced the phone in the cradle.

Jessica slumped down on her bed, feeling totally defeated. She had gotten just what she wanted. Devon and Elizabeth had broken up. And Elizabeth didn't want to have anything to do with either of the boys. Jessica's plan had succeeded perfectly.

But here she was, all alone. Devon hated her. Todd was angry at her. And Elizabeth never wanted to speak to her again. Was revenge really so sweet?

Now that she's seen Todd's and Devon's true colors, is Elizabeth through with love for good? Find out in Sweet Valley High #140: **Please Forgive Me.**

Bantam Books in the Sweet Valley High series
Ask your bookseller for the books you have missed

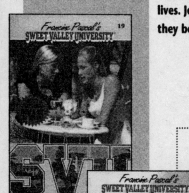

You'll always remember your first love.

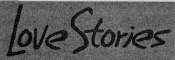

Looking for signs he's ready to fall in love? Want the guy's point of view? Then you should check out the  **Love Stories series. Romantic stories that tell it like it is— why he doesn't call, how to ask him out, when to say good-bye.**

BFYR 135